Raves For the Work of JASON STARR!

"Starr has…a hard-edged style that is clean, cold and extremely chilling."
—*New York Times*

"A throwback to the spare, snappy crime writing of Jim Thompson and James M. Cain."
—*Entertainment Weekly*

"Jason Starr is the first writer of his generation to convincingly update the modern crime novel."
—*Bret Easton Ellis*

"A fearless, pitiless writer."
—*Laura Lippman*

"The New York sound, the energy, dialog that's on the beat…Read it and you'll go hunting for Jason Starr's other books, I promise."
—*Elmore Leonard*

"[A] crackling hot beach read."
—*New York Post*

"Diabolically well-plotted."
—*The Literary Review*

"Deliciously addictive."
—*Megan Abbott*

We started to make out again, then she was lying on the couch on her back and I was on top of her. I pulled back and smiled, looking into her eyes, and then we went into the bedroom.

Afterwards, her head was wedged between my arm and my chest. We were naked and sweaty.

"It feels so nice to be with you," she said.

A few minutes later she was fast asleep.

I noticed the jewelry box on the dresser. I got out of bed and dressed quietly. The light on the night table was still on. In the dim yellow light I saw Janene still facing the other way. A necklace and a bracelet were out next to the jewelry box, but she'd probably notice if they were missing. Instead, I reached inside the box and took out another necklace, some diamond earrings, and a gold bracelet. I put the jewelry in my pocket. Janene was still fast asleep. I tiptoed out of the room and left the apartment...

FAKE I.D.

by Jason Starr

A HARD CASE CRIME NOVEL

A HARD CASE CRIME BOOK
(HCC-056)
June 2009

Published by

Dorchester Publishing Co., Inc.
200 Madison Avenue
New York, NY 10016

in collaboration with Winterfall LLC

*This book is a work of fiction. Names, characters, places, and
incidents either are the products of the author's imagination or
are used fictitiously, and any resemblance to actual events or
persons, living or dead, is entirely coincidental.*

ISBN 0-8439-6118-X
ISBN-13 978-0-8439-6118-8

Cover design by Cooley Design Lab

Typeset by Swordsmith Productions

Printed in the United States of America

Visit us on the web at www.HardCaseCrime.com

For Sandy

FAKE I.D.

One

The gates to Milford Jai-Alai didn't open for another hour, but instead of driving to some diner to kill time, I figured I'd just hang out in my car, reading the *Racing Form*.

I had just started going over the daily double at Aqueduct when I heard someone knocking on my passenger-side window. I looked up and saw a short fat guy smiling at me. At first, I had no idea who he was, then he started to look familiar. He had dark eyebrows and a big mole on his chin. His eyes were bloodshot, like he was drunk, but maybe it was because he was squinting against the cold wind. He was wearing one of those black wool winter hats that can make anyone look like a mental patient.

I turned on the ignition and opened the window a few inches. A blast of cold air came into the car.

"How's it goin'?" the guy asked.

I still couldn't place him. He looked forty-five, maybe fifty—at least ten years older than me.

"Not bad," I said.

"You don't remember me, do you?"

"Your face looks kind of familiar but—"

"Your name's Danny, right?"

"Tommy," I said.

"I knew it was something with a Y at the end of it. Remember me? You know, Pete. Pete from Yonkers."

Now I remembered. A few years ago, I used to go to Yonkers Raceway a few nights a week to bet on the trotters. Pete was one of the regulars.

"I remember," I said. "It just took me a couple seconds to place your face. How's it going?"

"Could be better," he said. "Just came back from Vegas last night. Hit a few things, nothing too big. Shoulda gone to the Cayman Islands. Hear about those racebooks they got down there?"

"With the eight-percent payback."

"Un-fuckin'-believable. They give you eight percent back on all your action. If you're a big player you can't afford *not* to go there. I mean it might be a good idea to bring a gun with you into some of those joints, you know what I mean? But when you're playing horses what do you want, a classy time or eight percent back on your action?"

"I'd take the eight percent," I said.

"Damn fucking right you would," Pete said, "any serious player would." He turned away and spat. It was getting cold in the car with the window open.

"Ever been to Vegas?" Pete asked.

I shook my head.

"You're kiddin' me? You gotta go to Vegas, man. But casino gambling is a whole different ball game. When you're gambling in a casino you *want* class. You go to Vegas, whatever you do, don't go to Bally's. You want Bally's go down to Atlantic City and play at those Mickey Mouse tables they got there. You want a classy joint to spend a weekend, go to Caesar's Palace. Now *that's* a place they'll treat you like a fucking king. And I'm talkin' about service, not shows. You want shows you can turn on the fuckin' TV. You go to A.C.?"

"Once in a while," I said.

"I'm in A.C. almost every fucking weekend," Pete said. "Where do you hang out?"

"All over," I said.

"It's tough to go to A.C. after you've been to Vegas," Pete said. "That's like going back to a Chevy after you've driven a Porsche." He coughed. "Hey, you mind if I sit down in the car with you? I'm fuckin' freezing my balls off out here."

I was going to say no, make up some excuse, but I couldn't think of a good one. Besides, I had some time to kill and I had nothing better to do. Leaning across the seat, I lifted the door handle and said, "You gotta pull." Pete used all his might, but the door still wouldn't open. My car was such a piece of shit it was a miracle it had gotten me all the way to Connecticut. It was an '89 Taurus, but there were so many dents in it you had to be Mike Tyson to get in and out of the fucker.

"Harder," I said.

Pete tried a couple more times, then, finally, the door swung open. He sat down next to me and I almost passed out. I had B.O. once in a while, especially after I worked out in the gym in a tank top, but Pete reeked. I opened my window a crack, to let in some fresh, cold air, but it didn't help.

"What was I just saying?" Pete said. "That's right—

A.C. I usually stay by the Sands. A guy I know runs the junkets from Brooklyn—gets me a deal on the rooms. If we're ever going down on the same weekend, maybe I can get you into my room. They got two beds in those rooms and the other one just goes to waste. My bed goes to waste too. When you're in Vegas or A.C. who the fuck uses their bed? I mean unless you're getting laid, but nobody *sleeps* in their bed. The room's just a place to store your luggage for two nights."

"I don't mean to be rude or anything," I said, "but I was trying to just go over the card at Aqueduct here…"

"Yeah?" Pete said, not getting the hint. "You like anything?"

"Not really," I said, "but I was just hoping I could concentrate a little bit, you know?"

"*No problema*," Pete said. "I won't bother you any-more."

He leaned back and took a handkerchief out of his jeans' pocket. He coughed some more into it, then put it away. The smell in the car was getting worse.

For a little while, Pete stared out the window on his side of the car, taking deep breaths, then he turned back toward me and said, "So what do you do for a living?"

"I'm an actor," I said.

"Really?" He sounded surprised or impressed, I couldn't tell which. "In anything I've heard of?"

"Doubt it," I said.

"Come on. Try me."

"Just a few things here and there," I said. "Nothing too big."

"I imagine acting must be a tough biz," Pete said, "tough to make a living anyway. So what else you do?"

"What do you mean?"

"I mean I assume you don't make a living as an actor."

"Why do you assume that?"

"No offense—I mean I'm not trying to knock you. I'm sure you're great and everything. You look the part, that's for sure. Big, good-looking guy. But do you have—what do they call it—'a survival job?'"

"I work in a bar," I said.

"Really? Anyplace I know?"

"O'Reilley's." Then I said, "It's on First Avenue."

"The city," he said, like he thought I was trying to be a snob about it. "So what do you do up there?"

"I'm a bouncer," I said.

"No kiddin'?" He stared at me for a second or two. "So you live in the city?"

"I got a little place near the bar."

"Yeah? You must make a few dollars at this job, huh?"

Now I was starting to get pissed off. Who the hell did this guy think he was, asking about my salary?

"I hold my own," I said.

"What do you work, five, six nights a week?"

I worked six nights a week like a fucking dog.

"Why are you asking all these questions?"

"I'm just curious," he said. "Believe me, I don't mean any offense by it."

"My salary is my own business."

"Believe me, I realize that. I don't really care how much money you make. The only reason I asked is I'm a businessman, and my friends are businessmen, and I just thought if you had any extra cash lying around your apartment—"

"I don't lend money," I said.

He started to laugh. The laugh turned into a deep cough.

"Please," he said, catching his breath. "Do I really look like I need your money?"

Yeah, I thought.

"I just wanted to find out what kind of income you had because an investment opportunity came my way recently and I figured a guy like you might be interested."

"I told you, I don't lend."

"This isn't lending, it's investing. Lemme explain." He wiped his mouth with the back of his hand, then said, "See, I know this guy—Alan Schwartz. You know, Jewish guy. Anyway, Schwartz works down on Wall Street and he's starting up this syndicate. Not one of those big-time syndicates that own Derby horses—this is just a bunch of guys putting some money together to buy a horse, or a couple of horses. The idea was to put five guys together—guys who love horse racing—and they'll go down to the track and buy a claimer. At first, I didn't trust the guy—I mean I'm not stupid. But then I checked it out and it was all legit. They have a trainer lined up and everything. You heard of Bill Tucker?"

I nodded.

"I met Bill a couple of weeks ago," Pete said. "Nice Southern, grits-and-collard-greens type of guy. Anyway, he's gonna advise us on what horse to claim and we'll see what happens. Who knows? We might wind up with another John Henry."

I knew the John Henry story—how he was claimed for twenty grand and went on to win millions—but I just sat there, staring.

"Anyway," Pete went on, "that's why I asked you how much money you were making. Not because I was being nosy, but because we have four guys lined up right now and we're looking for a fifth. Each guy is putting up ten grand. I don't know if that's in your ball-park or not, or if you even want to own part of a horse, but I figured it couldn't hurt to ask."

The whole thing sounded like a big scam to me. Asking a stranger in a parking lot to join a horse syndi-cate? Obviously, Pete was just a con man, trying to sucker me out of some money, and I wasn't the type of guy who got suckered.

"Sorry," I said. "Not interested."

"Just thought I'd ask," Pete said. "Figured a racing fan like yourself would love to get in on the ground floor of something like this, but I'm sure we'll find somebody else. Hey, if you're ever in Brooklyn make sure you stop by one of my stores. I'll give you an actor's discount."

"Your stores?"

"Didn't I tell you? I own a couple of shoe stores out in Brooklyn. You know Kings Highway?"

"I grew up in Brooklyn."

"No shit? I heard an accent, but I thought it might be Staten Island or Jersey. Where you from?"

"Canarsie."

"You're shitting me? I grew up in Coney Island, by Neptune Avenue. Now I live in Manhattan Beach. Got a big house, right by the water. Anyway, I got two stores in Brooklyn. The main one's on Kings Highway. It's called Logan's after me—Pete Logan."

I'd bought a pair of shoes at Logan's when I was in high school, and now I remembered Pete. I could picture him, twenty years ago, standing behind the register, or he might've been the guy who sold me the shoes.

"Anyway," he said, "just drop by one of my stores next time you're in the neighborhood. If I'm not there just mention my name and you'll get the discount. It was nice running into you again."

I watched Pete walk across the parking lot and get into a shiny black Mercedes. So the guy owned some shoe stores and he drove a Merc, that didn't mean he wasn't a scammer.

I tried to get back to reading my *Racing Form*, but I couldn't concentrate. It was that odor. My damn car smelled like somebody had died in it.

Two

Of course I couldn't catch a break at jai-alai. The sport was so fixed I always felt like a sucker the second the teller printed my tickets. After losing two games in a row I ripped up my program and went to play horses and dogs in the simulcast area in the back of the fronton.

Usually, when I didn't have any auditions to go to which was pretty much all the time these days—and when I wasn't working at the bar, I hung out at the OTB or at the Inside Track Teletheater on Fifty-third Street. Today I'd thought it would be nice to gamble someplace else for a change, but the way things were going in another hour I'd be back on the Turnpike, on my way back to the city.

I wasn't hungry, but I decided I needed something to bite into, to let out my aggravation, so I got on line to buy a hamburger. A few seconds later, I turned around and saw Pete, standing at the counter, squirting catsup onto a hot dog. I made a U-turn, heading toward where they were showing the dog races. I knew I couldn't dodge him forever. The place wasn't very big and if they were lucky they had three hundred people today.

I never won betting on dogs, but I opened the Plain-field program anyway. I bet fifty to win on the number

five and then watched the five get wiped out by another
dog on the first turn. Cursing, ripping up the ticket, I
went back to the concession stand and saw that Pete
was gone. Thank fuckin' God. After I downed two
burgers, I counted my money. I had $216 in my wallet,
but I had to save at least twenty bucks for gas and tolls
back to the city. I decided that I'd bet a hundred on
the horse I liked in the second at Aqueduct and play
with whatever money I had left for the rest of the day.

I went to the bathroom and took a leak. I was by
the sink, splashing cold water against my face, when
I looked straight ahead, into the mirror, and saw
Pete coming up behind me. In the bright fluorescent
light the mole on his chin looked bigger, and the hairs
growing out of it were darker. He wasn't wearing his
wool cap anymore. His black and gray hair was curly
and messy.

"How's it goin'?" he asked.

"All right," I said.

"I was looking for you before," he said. "I couldn't
find you anywhere so I figured you took off."

I unwound some paper towel and started wiping
my face.

"I'm still here," I said.

"I can see that," he said. "So how you doing? Catch
any winners so far?"

I didn't want to tell him that I was losing my balls.

"Hit a few things," I said.

"Wish I could say the same," Pete said.

"Your luck's gotta change eventually."

"So where you hanging out?" Pete asked. "Maybe I'll come by and visit."

"I'm just walking around a lot," I said. "I'm not sitting anywhere."

Now I could tell he got the hint.

"Whatever," he said. "Maybe we'll bump into each other later on."

In the mirror, I watched Pete leave the bathroom.

I bet the Aqueduct race, putting one hundred to win on the ten horse and then I bet another fifty in exactas with the ten on top of a few other horses. The ten broke good out of the gate, then dropped back and closed late, missing by a head. I screamed at the TV and kicked a garbage can so hard a security guard came over and told me if I did that again he'd have to toss me.

Now I only had sixty-six dollars left, including gas-and-toll money. I knew this wouldn't be enough to last me the rest of the day so I got on line at the ATM to take money off my Visa card. There were four guys ahead of me. They looked like degenerates, wearing dirty jeans, sneakers, and old winter jackets. Then I thought, How was I any better? Wasn't I on the same line, waiting to take money off *my* credit card? A couple of minutes ago I probably looked like even more of a loser, kicking that garbage can and screaming like a maniac.

I only had sixty-four dollars left on the card so I took out an even sixty, figuring it would last me another couple of races. There was no doubt about it now—I wasn't winning today. In a couple of hours I'd be back home, in my living room, watching TV. Then, at six o'clock, I'd be back at work—another exciting night of sitting on a bar stool, checking IDs.

After I lost the third at Aqueduct, I started looking over the rest of the card. Now it wasn't a matter of if, but how I'd lose—and then I looked up from my *Form*, at the TV screen. The winner of the Aqueduct race was in the winner's circle. The jockey was off the horse, standing between two guys in suits, probably the trainer and the owner. Next to the guy on the right was a good-looking blonde in a white dress and high heels.

Every racing fan dreams of owning a horse someday, just like every Little Leaguer dreams about playing in the majors. I always figured that after I became a famous actor, I'd own a whole stable of horses out at Hollywood Park in California. A lot of famous actors owned race horses and I'd always imagined myself going to the track with my girlfriend—some model or actress I was dating—and sitting in an owner's box, watching my horses run.

But the way things were going I had a better chance of hitting Lotto than I did of making it as an actor. My manager hardly sent me out on casting calls anymore and I couldn't blame him. He had to eat too, and I'd probably gone to at least five hundred auditions over the past nine years and I only got two parts—an understudy in some Off-Broadway play that closed after six performances, and a bit role in a kung fu movie that went straight to video. I did some extra work, when it was available, and I used to do a little catalog modeling, but lately I hadn't gotten any work at all. It was always the same story—whenever I went to auditions for "big dark guys with blue eyes," there'd be a hundred actors there who looked just like me. It was like being in a house of mirrors—looking around, seeing myself everywhere.

Six years ago, I almost had my big break. I screen tested to be in a romantic comedy with Melanie Griffith. The director, guy named Simon Devaux, loved me. I met Devaux at his penthouse on the West Side and he told me I reminded him of a young Brando. He said after this movie came out I was going to be one of the hottest stars in Hollywood, that I'd be able to write my own paychecks.

The day before I was supposed to fly out to the coast to meet with the producers and Melanie, my manager called me and said he had some bad news. I thought he was going to say my flight was canceled, but then he said no, it was a lot worse than that—Simon Devaux was dead. He drove off a cliff in Big Sur, on his way to L.A. from San Francisco. I felt like it was all some sick joke. I was so close to making it, then, all of a sudden, the dream was dead again. My manager told me not to worry about it—other offers would start coming in— but so far that hadn't happened, and it was getting harder and harder to stay positive.

If I didn't make it as an actor I had no idea what I'd do with the rest of my life. I did two years at Brooklyn College, but I couldn't see myself going back to school —not at thirty-two years old. One thing for sure, I wasn't going to be a bouncer forever. If I was forty and I was still sitting on a bar stool every night, I was going to stick a gun in my mouth and blow my brains out. I needed a back-up plan—something to do when my acting career fell apart for good.

I went toward the front of the fronton, out to the grandstand. I walked up and down the aisle a few times, looking for Pete in the stands, but I didn't see him anywhere. I started to walk faster, looking around in every direction. I looked all over the building—in the bathroom, in the simulcast area, near the concession stands. I was about to go outside and look for his car in the lot, when I saw him walking away from one of the betting windows. I jogged toward him, reaching him right at the entrance to the grandstand.

When I called out his name he turned around. He didn't exactly look happy to see me.

"I was looking around for you all over the place," I said. "I thought you might've taken off."

"Why were you looking for me?" he asked.

"Just wanted to say hello," I said. "I also wanted to say sorry for before. I was a real asshole."

The lights in the grandstand dimmed, and the usual loud trumpet music came on as the jai-alai players marched on to the court for the next game.

"I don't want to miss the game," Pete said.

"I'll come watch it with you," I said. "Where you sitting?"

"I got a reserved seat—up front."

"The usher won't bust my balls if I sit with you for

one game," I said. "I mean they have what, fifty people here today?"

I could tell that Pete was still pissed off, but he motioned with his head for me to come sit with him anyway.

We sat in the center section, in the fourth row. The elevated court was at eye level, and we had a head-on view of the game through the mesh that separated the players and the stands. Pete still smelled, but for some reason it didn't bother me anymore.

"So who do you got here?" I asked.

"The one in exotics," Pete said.

"I'll root you home," I said.

The one served to start the game. The two hit a weak shot back that the one put away for an easy *chula*.

"That's one," I said, but Pete wasn't looking at me.

The one took another point from the three, then lost to the four, hitting an easy shot right into the mesh. As usual, the game looked completely fixed and some people in the crowd started to boo.

"You'll get' em in the next round," I said.

As we watched the four play the five I said, "So I was thinking about what you told me before—I mean in the car outside—about buying into a share of that horse. I was wondering if you could tell me a little more about that."

"I thought you weren't interested," Pete said. He sounded pissed off again, but I didn't think it had to do with me anymore. He was probably still mad about the one missing that easy shot.

"Yeah, well I've been giving it a little more thought," I said. "I was thinking it might be kind of fun to own a piece of a race horse."

The five missed an easy shot to give the four his second point. The whole crowd booed.

"It has to beat coming down here," I said, "throwing your money away on these crooks."

Pete smiled. I could tell he forgave me completely now for the way I had acted in the bathroom.

"The only problem is it's a big risk," Pete said. "Hopefully, we'll make some money, but chances are we're just throwing away ten grand apiece. The only reason I asked you to come on board in the first place was because I didn't know what you did for a living. I thought you might have some expendable income or—what do the stockbrokers call it?—risk capital. But if you're gonna have to go out on a limb—"

"Money's no problem," I lied. "I just wanted to know more details about it. You know, the way the contract works and shit like that."

"I don't have all the details with me," Pete said. "But if you're telling me you're interested in this, Alan Schwartz, the Jewish guy I was talking about, can give you all the info. He has this package he printed up—you know, a prospectus. It explains how it all works. But I need to know one hundred percent because Alan's a big-time Wall Street guy and I don't want to waste his time."

"I'll have to think it over," I said. "How about I let you know for sure in a day or two?"

"The sooner the better," Pete said. "We're looking

to find somebody else by the end of the week. For all I know Alan already found somebody."

The four made a great play, climbing the side wall to pull down a shot, then he backhanded a *chula*. A few people cheered.

"You're right to stay away from this bullshit," Pete said to me. "I have to be out of my mind, throwing my money away on these fucking *banditos*."

"There's just one thing I'm still wondering about," I said, hardly paying attention to the game, "but I don't want you to take this the wrong way."

"Shoot," Pete said.

"You own Logan's shoe stores so you must have some serious money. Why don't you just buy a horse on your own? Or, if you don't want to buy a whole horse, why don't you just buy the fifth share for another ten grand? Why do you have to go find somebody else?"

Pete smiled, like he was thinking about some old joke, then said, "You kiddin' me? I'd love to own a horse myself, and if I had my way I'd own a whole stable of horses someday. But you can't just jump into the horse business overnight. You have to know what you're doing, you need contacts. That's why I figured I'd go in on this syndicate. Alan Schwartz knows the trainers, knows all that shit. I figured it would show me the ropes, then I go out and start buying my own horses. But the reason I can't put up the other ten grand—because, believe me, I would if I could— is Alan wants us all to be even owners, twenty percent a piece. He's afraid if one guy got forty percent of the horse he'd start making all the decisions and he's right. This way, with five guys, we vote on everything and the majority rules."

Pete was checking his tickets, ripping them up one by one.

"That's it for me," he said. "I've given these assholes enough of my money for one afternoon."

"Taking off?"

"Maybe I'll hit Yonkers on my way back to Brooklyn," he said. "See how I feel."

I was thinking about asking Pete if he wanted some company at the trotters, but then I remembered how I was almost broke and how I didn't even have any money left on my credit cards. So instead I said, "So how do I get in touch with you when I make up my mind?"

Pete dug into his pocket and took out a thick wallet. From one of the compartments he slid out a business card and handed it to me. "This is my card, but it's not me you're gonna have to talk to, it's Alan. I'm gonna give you his work number. If he's not there leave a message on his voice mail and tell him I told you to call. But don't call him if you're not serious. Alan's a busy guy—he doesn't fuck around."

I looked at the front of the business card and saw the little picture of a shoe—the logo of Logan's shoe stores—then the listing of the two locations in Brooklyn. PETE LOGAN, OWNER was printed in bold lettering across the top of the card. On the back of the card he'd written a phone number and "Alan Schwartz," underlined twice.

I shook Pete's sweaty hand, then I watched him walk

up the aisle toward the exit. I pissed the rest of my money away on a couple of dog races and a few minutes later I was back on the Turnpike.

I was driving in the right lane, going about forty. I took out Pete's card and put it on the dashboard. It looked like a real business card, but how hard would it be to print up some business cards saying you own the Logan's shoe stores in Brooklyn? The whole thing could've been the old "give and take away" routine. Tell a guy he can have something, like a share of a horse, then when he wants it tell him he might not be able to have it and that makes him want it even more. Why else would Pete have said that they could've "already found somebody." In the parking lot, he made it sound like the whole thing was up to me, then, all of a sudden, it wasn't.

I put on the radio on WFAN, listening to Mike and the Mad Dog talking about the Jets' playoff chances. A tractor trailer ahead of me moved into my lane, cutting me off.

"Motherfucker!" I yelled, braking hard. The business card shifted on the dashboard, almost falling down the heating grate.

"Jesus," I said.

I took the card off the dashboard and put it away in my wallet for safekeeping.

Three

I lived in a one-room walkup on Sixty-fourth Street between First and York. Frank, my boss at work, had fixed me up with a friend of his, a Greek guy named Costas, who owned some buildings in the neighborhood. There was no super in the building so Costas cut a deal with me—he gave me a break on the rent for taking care of the building. Nothing too fancy—I had to take out the garbage, fix leaky sinks, put down glue traps and roach baits. Sometimes it was a big pain in the ass but the rent was so cheap—four-eighty a month in a neighborhood where studios went for twelve hundred easy—it was worth it.

The only problem was the apartment was built for a midget—two hundred and fifty square feet and when they said "square feet" they meant it. It was like I was living in a jail cell, with a little kitchenette in one corner, a door to a small bathroom in another, and a pull-out couch in the corner to the left of where you walked in. The place was always a mess—covered with dirty laundry, newspaper, junk mail and other garbage. Dishes were piled up in the sink and I couldn't remember the last time I'd washed a piece of silverware. I tried to keep it clean, but in a place so small it was impossible. I couldn't decorate for shit so I didn't even try. I didn't know what to do with one wall so I banged some nails into it and hung up some old baseball caps. On another wall was a big poster of DeNiro in *Raging Bull*. Next to the poster was my latest eight-by-ten head shot—smiling, with the collar of my leather jacket flipped up like Travolta in *Grease*. There was never anything to eat in the fridge and I didn't know how to cook anyway. I either ate my meals at the bar or ordered in.

The apartment might have been small, but it was a palace compared to some of the other places I'd lived. When I first moved to the city, after I left college, I had a job working in the kitchen at a Chinese restaurant on the Lower East Side. I was living in a small, run-down apartment above the restaurant with four Chinese guys. I slept on a mat on the floor and I woke up one night and there was a family of rats crawling on me. My other apartments weren't much better— roach-infested shitholes without heat or hot water that probably should have been condemned by the Board of Health. When I was younger, where I lived never seemed to matter because I always knew it was tempo- rary, that I'd eventually make it as an actor and then look back at my time when I was struggling as "the good old days." I'd be interviewed on *Access Hollywood* or *Entertainment Tonight* and tell my rat story and every- one would laugh, like it was all a big joke. But, lately, I'd been getting tired of struggling. I wanted to live in a nice apartment and have money in the bank and I wanted it to happen soon.

I took off all my clothes, letting them drop onto the floor. I was famished, but I remembered that I was almost broke. I still had three dollars and some change left over from my toll-and-gas money. In the pockets of my coats and pants I found some more change, including a crumpled dollar, and I found sixty-eight cents under the couch cushions. Out of places to look, I counted all the money I'd found—five dollars and sixteen cents. It wasn't even enough to order a hero from Pizza Park on First Avenue, unless I wanted to stiff the kid on the tip.

I thought about taking a walk around the corner, buying a couple of slices and a Coke and calling it dinner, but I decided it wasn't worth freezing my ass off. Instead, I figured I'd just hold out a couple of hours until I went to work.

Sitting in front of the TV, flipping channels without paying attention to what was on, I decided I had to be crazy to even take Pete's business card home with me. How could I come up with ten grand when I couldn't even scrounge up enough money to order a pizza? Besides, I was an actor. Acting had been my dream since I was a kid. My mother and father were rough on me a lot, so I spent hours in my room alone with the door locked, looking at myself in the mirror, repeating the lines I'd heard on TV and in the movies over and over again. When I grew up, I wanted to be just like DeNiro in *Taxi Driver* or Pacino in *Scarface*. In high school, I had lead roles in all the productions and my drama teacher, Mrs. Warren, told me I had "can't-miss talent." I couldn't quit now, just because things weren't going my way. I had an audition tomorrow afternoon for a part in a dog food commercial. After I got that role, I'd land a part in a soap and then the movie people would start calling. Maybe it would take a little longer to get to Hollywood than I'd thought, but I'd get there eventually. I knew I had too much talent to go unnoticed forever.

I put on my usual work outfit—faded jeans, a tight black crew-neck T-shirt, my chain with a little gold barbell that I'd had since high school, and black motorcycle boots. Wearing my long black leather coat unbuttoned, I left my apartment.

O'Reilley's was only a couple of blocks away on First Avenue between Sixty-fifth and Sixty-sixth. When I arrived, a few regulars were sitting at the bar by themselves. Like a lot of bars in Manhattan, O'Reilley's had its "day crowd" and its "night crowd." The day crowd was old men, construction workers, electricians, carpenters, and plain drunks. They came to drink hard liquor and to get away from their wives and bosses. Late in the afternoon, toward five, the day crowd started thinning out, and then the younger happy-hour crowd arrived. O'Reilley's wasn't a big-time happy-hour bar—we got about twenty people on a typical night—so I didn't do much proofing at the door until the night crowd arrived, usually around eight or nine. Until then, I sometimes helped out at the bar, or I hung around doing nothing. I had to admit that, even though being a bouncer wasn't the most exciting job in the world, at least it was easy. It beat the hell out of washing dishes and waiting tables and driving cabs and all the other shit jobs I'd had. Basically, all I had to do was sit on a bar stool and look tough. Once in a while, on Friday and Saturday nights, a guy would drink a few beers and turn into a big shot. Usually, it would be two guys fighting each other and I'd go in and break it up. A couple of times drunk guys took swings at me and I had to get a little rough, but I hated when that happened. I wasn't one of those asshole bouncers who lived for the days I had to hit people. If two guys wanted to go at it I always let them go, as long as it wasn't inside the bar.

One of the perks of being a bouncer at a bar on the Upper East Side was that I met a lot of good-looking women. Girls were always coming up to me at the door, starting conversations. The underage ones were just trying to kiss up to me so I'd let them into the bar, and other ones were just trying to scam free drinks. But a lot of them really liked me too, giving me their phone numbers without me even asking. I went out with a lot of the girls I met at work, and had sex with some of them, but I'd never had a relationship that lasted for more than a month.

I was hoping Frank, my boss, was around so I could hit him up for an advance on my salary. Sometimes Frank bartended for the day crowd but his son, Gary, was working the bar.

I was on my way to the back, to hang up my coat, when a hand touched my shoulder. I turned around and Kathy was standing there, smiling, holding a plate with a burger and fries.

"Tommy, I'm so glad you're here—I have some amazing news to tell you."

"You brought me my dinner?"

"Seriously. I'll be right back."

I watched her bring the plate over to a guy sitting at the bar. Kathy was a twenty-five-year-old aspiring actress. Last year, when she first started working at O'Reilley's, we had a one-night stand. She was tall and thin with long straight brown hair. I guess most guys would think she was beautiful, but she wasn't really my type. I never understood why some women starved themselves, trying to look like the models in magazines. To me, nothing was sexier than a woman with a nice stomach and big thighs.

Kathy came back smiling and hugged me and kissed me on the cheek. Then she said, "So you won't believe it. Remember that audition I told you I was going to last week? You know, the one for the new Terrence McNally play at the Manhattan Theatre Club?"

"Yeah," I said.

"Well, I got a callback. Isn't that unbelievable? And my agent says they don't fool around at the MTC. If you get a callback, they really like you."

"That's great," I said. I was happy for her, but I really wasn't in the mood to hear about how somebody else's acting career was taking off.

"I'm not gonna get my hopes up though—I mean I don't want to jinx it or anything. But I really love this part and I know I can do it. But I wanted to talk to you about something else. It was something my agent suggested actually. He thought it might be a good idea if I did a showcase with another actor—you know, a scene or a one-act play—and my agent says he'll get some directors and producers to come down and watch it. And, I don't know what you think, but I thought it might be fun if you and me, I don't know, did a scene or something together."

"Sounds like a good idea to me," I said.

"Great!" she said. "I was thinking about this play called *Police Story*. It's an old play from the fifties. Anyway, it's a really good police drama and there are some really good husband-and-wife scenes in it. If you liked it too, maybe we could try it. I'll go to the drama library at Lincoln Center tomorrow and see if anything else looks good. I'm so nervous."

Kathy went to take somebody else's order and I went to the back and hung up my coat. I was starving and if I didn't eat something soon I was going to pass out. I went into the kitchen and had Rodrigo cook me a well-done burger, loaded with onions and relish, with a side of onion rings. I stood in the kitchen, bullshitting with him until the food was done. Rodrigo was a short Mexican guy with a thick black mustache. He was trying to learn English and I helped him out whenever I could. Today he was trying to learn how to ask his landlord for more heat. I got a piece of paper and wrote out exactly what he should tell him.

"Thank you, Tommy," Rodrigo said. "Now my wife and me—we don't freeze."

I took the burger with me to the bar. Pat Benatar was singing "Hit Me With Your Best Shot" and I was singing along, suddenly in a better mood. I reached over and poured myself a pint of Sam Adams and then I started to wolf down my food. The burger was okay—

not as well-done as I liked—but it could've been raw meat and I would've eaten it.

At the other end of the bar, Gary was having a conversation with one of the old-timers. Gary was the only person at O'Reilley's I didn't get along with. I didn't have anything against him, but he didn't like me because his father gave me special treatment. Frank was always telling Gary that he was throwing away his life, trying to be a rock star and smoking pot, and he wanted him to go back to college. I pretty much agreed with Frank about Gary. I knew I shouldn't be the one to talk because my career wasn't exactly skyrocketing, but at least I was a pretty good actor—I wasn't just wasting my time. Sometimes Gary played his band's demo tape and I couldn't believe how bad they sucked. They sounded like a high school band, practicing in somebody's garage. Besides, when you're in your thirties you still have a shot of making it as an actor, but anybody who turns on MTV knows that all the hot new rock stars are in their twenties. Gary was thirty-four, two years older than me, and his band was still playing in bars—not even bars, in *coffee* bars—in the East Village.

Gary was tall, thin and very pale. He dressed like your typical wannabe rock star, in skin-tight leather pants and ripped T-shirts. He wore silver hoop earrings and he had blond streaks dyed into his straight brown hair. I had never seen him with a girl and I was pretty sure he was gay.

I finished my burger. I was still hungry, but the food would hold me over for a while.

"Hey, Gary," I called down the bar. "Your father coming in tonight?"

Gary shook his head.

"Why not?" I asked.

"Said he's not feeling well. Why?"

"Forget it," I said. "It's no big deal."

I didn't know what I was going to do. I could get by without money for tonight, but I still needed some money to live on and it would probably be a good idea if I paid my rent and some bills eventually. If Frank didn't show up tomorrow I'd be in serious trouble.

A girl came into the bar. I watched her take her coat off, spread it over a stool two stools away from me, then sit down. She looked over at me and smiled and I smiled back. She looked like she was coming from work—wearing a short black skirt and a black blouse. Gary took her order—"A frozen margarita please"— and then she crossed her legs. I took another look— wavy dark hair, dark skin, probably Indian—and then I slid over one stool, held out my hand, and said, "Pleasure to meet you, I'm Tommy." We shook hands and started talking. She told me her name, but it was something Indian I didn't understand. It sounded like she'd said "Tree Lips," but I knew that couldn't be it. I have no idea what we talked about, but she was laughing so I figured she must like me.

After a while, I asked her if she was waiting for somebody. "Actually, I am," she said, looking toward the door. "I'm waiting for a friend." I asked for her phone number and she hit me with the old "I have a boyfriend" line. I knew it couldn't be too serious—she was wearing rings on every finger on her left hand *except* her ring finger. I could have pushed it, seen if she was just playing hard to get, but I wasn't in the mood. When the friend showed up I told Tree Lips that it was very nice meeting her and that I hoped we had a chance to hang out again sometime. Then the girls went to sit down at a table and I reached across the bar and poured myself another pint of Sam Adams.

"Why did you tell her you're an actor?"

I looked up and Gary was across the bar from me.

"Who asked you?" I said.

"I just couldn't help overhearing what you were saying," he said. "I mean you were talking so *loud*."

I took a sip of beer, ignoring him.

"You don't hear me telling people I'm a musician," he went on. "When people ask me what I do for a living I say I'm a bartender."

"You *are* a bartender."

"And *you're* a bouncer."

"No, I'm an actor."

"No, what you are is what you get *paid* to do. Until you're working full-time as an actor you're a bouncer and acting is just a hobby. You shouldn't be afraid to be who you are."

"Thanks for the advice," I said.

I took the beer with me to the other end of the bar and finished it in a few gulps. Then I went outside to check IDs.

*

It was a normal Wednesday night until around ten-thirty when Janene walked in with two friends. I'd met Janene at the door about a month ago. On one of my nights off I took her out to dinner at Carmine's on Forty-fourth Street and then we went back to my place and she spent the night. I hadn't called her since and I felt bad about it now. I'd had a great time with her—she was nice, good looking, fun to talk to—what the hell was wrong with me? Naturally, she was giving me the silent treatment tonight. She said hi to me at the door, but she didn't smile, and now she was standing with her friends at the bar, pretending not to notice me.

I kept looking over at her. No doubt about it—she was spectacular. Her dirty blond hair was cut to a shoulder-length bob and she was wearing tight jeans and a blue wool sweater. She was thirty-one but she looked twenty-five. She was a big girl—about five-ten, one-eighty—just my type.

When it got slow at the door I went over to the bar and started talking to her. I'd forgotten how beautiful her eyes were. They were bright blue and always seemed to sparkle. I also noticed her negative body language, how she wouldn't turn her shoulder toward me, but I kept bullshitting with her anyway.

Then, out of nowhere, she said, "So why didn't you call me?"

I'd been expecting this question and I was ready with an answer.

"I was planning to," I said. "I've just been really busy lately."

"Whatever," she said, pretending she didn't care, but it was obvious she did. "I just don't get it, though. I mean I thought we had a good time together."

"We *did* have a good time together. At least I know I did."

"Then why didn't you call me? And don't tell me you were busy. How long does it take to make a phone call?"

Looking down I said, "I guess I didn't think you liked me that much."

"Come on," she said. "You're kidding, right?"

"I've heard a lot of girls talking—about how when they sleep with a guy on the first date it means they don't really care about the guy—what he thinks of them."

"That's crazy," she said. "What do you think I do, sleep with every guy I go out with?"

A guy standing behind Janene, drinking a bottle of beer, looked over at us.

"I know I was wrong," I said, "I should've called you. But I just wanted to tell you what was going on in my mind, that's all."

"And what do you think I thought after I didn't hear from you?"

"We had a misunderstanding then—what can I say? But I really am sorry. Believe me I had a great time with you—it was probably one of the best dates I've ever had. I'd really like to hang out with you again sometime, but if you don't want to I'd understand."

"I don't know," she said. "I guess I'll have to think it over."

"Fair enough," I said, "but believe me, I won't let you down again—you can count on that." I started to leave, then I looked back at her and said, "And, by the way, I just want to tell you—you look great tonight."

"I do?" She was blushing.

"Come on, you know you do."

She was looking down.

"Look," I said, "I'm gonna get off at one-thirty tonight. If you feel like it, maybe you want to stick around. We could go out for a late drink somewhere— or just get some coffee. We could just talk, you know, see how it goes."

"Maybe," she said.

We made some more eye contact, then I said, "You know where to find me."

I went back to my stool by the door. While I was working, every now and then, I looked over in Janene's direction and when she saw me we both smiled. I had a feeling I was winning her back, but I couldn't tell for sure. Then, around one o'clock, she came over to me and said, "My friends are going home."

"What about you?"

"I told them I have a date with the bouncer."

Lying next to Janene in the dark I said, "I wish I could offer you something to drink, but all I have is tap water."

"That's all right."

"You sure? Because I could run out and get something—I don't mind."

"No. Really."

I ran my fingers gently down her forehead then over the side of her face.

"Anybody ever tell you you have beautiful skin?"

"You're always complimenting me."

"Is something wrong with that?"

"I guess not."

"It's so soft and smooth—like a nectarine."

"Thank you," she said laughing.

I kissed her, then I reached across her body to turn on the lamp.

"What are you doing?"

"I want to see your face."

"Don't."

"Why not?"

"Because...I guess I'm just a little insecure, that's all."

"What do you have to be insecure about?"

"My legs."

"Jesus, women always think there's one thing wrong with them and it's always the most attractive part of their body. All right, give it to me. What's wrong with your legs?"

"They're fat."

"Fat? They're not fat enough. If you put another ten pounds on each of them they'd be perfect."

"Thanks, but keep the light off please."

She grabbed my arms and then we started wrestling, rolling around on the bed. When I was on top of her, kissing her, she said, "Tommy, I want to ask you a question?"

"Shoot," I said with my lips against hers.

"If I didn't come into the bar tonight would you ever've called me?"

"Probably," I said. I was kissing her neck now. In between kisses I said, "I know I was thinking about you a lot."

"What were you thinking?"

"Just wondering about you, hoping you weren't with some other guy, that you were thinking about me too."

"I was—thinking about you too, I mean. A lot. That's why I was so disappointed when you didn't call."

"You're gonna hold that against me forever, huh?"

"No, it's just I feel so lucky now. I mean I can't believe I met a nice guy like you. You have no idea how many losers and assholes there are out there. But I also feel bad about something."

"What's that?"

"That we…you know…again. I mean maybe we should be taking it slower."

"That's crazy," I said. "I like you and you like me, right? So why shouldn't we enjoy ourselves?"

"You know what I mean. I'm afraid you're going to get tired of me."

"Impossible." I rolled over, pulling her on top of me. She was crazy, worrying about her legs. Her legs were perfect.

"Tommy, can I ask you something else?"

"You can ask me anything you want."

She twirled her index finger around in my chest hair.

"What do you see yourself doing someday?" she asked. "I mean if you can't be an actor."

"But I *am* an actor."

"You know what I mean—if acting as a career doesn't work out for you. What else would you want to do?"

I wasn't in the mood for this—especially after Gary gave me the needles this afternoon. It was hard enough getting turned down for part after part by producers and directors—I didn't need other people shooting me down. But I didn't want to get mad at Janene either. Things were going too good tonight and I wanted to keep it that way.

"It sounds like you have a problem with dating a bouncer," I said.

"No, that's not it at all. I'm just curious. I'm not trying to put pressure on you or anything. I'm sorry, I guess I should've kept my mouth shut."

"It's all right," I said. "I just don't like to think about the possibility of not making it, that's all. The power of positive thinking, you know? But, all right, if we're talking 'what if,' I've always been pretty good with numbers. I figure if my acting career fell apart I could always get a job down on Wall Street, join one of those stockbroker training programs I always see ads for in the paper."

"I think you'd make a *great* stockbroker."

"Or maybe I'd do something else—go into sales or management. Or—who knows—maybe I'll own race horses."

"*Race horses?*"

"You know what I mean—there're a lot of things I can do. Don't worry, I won't be a bouncer forever."

Janene had started running her fingers through my hair.

"What's that?" she asked, squinting, looking at my scalp.

"Just my scar," I said.

"How'd you get it?"

"Fell off a bike when I was a kid."

"It must've been a bad fall."

"Nah, I just needed a few stitches to sew it up. It was no big deal."

I always told "the bike accident story" whenever a girl or a barber asked about my scar. It was better than telling the real story of how I was hurt and explaining how, when I was seven years old, I'd had to have a chunk of my skull removed and replaced with a metal plate.

But I liked Janene a lot and I planned to tell her the truth about the scar and everything else about me eventually.

We made love again slowly, talking and laughing the whole time. I couldn't believe how comfortable I felt around Janene, like I'd known her for years.

Then, lying next to each other again, she rested her head on my sweaty chest and said, "I have to tell you something important."

"What is it?"

She didn't say anything.

"Well?"

"Never mind," she finally said. "I'll tell you some other time."

"I thought you said it's important."

"It is, but it can wait."

"Is it something I should be worried about?"

"No, it's nothing like *that*. Forget it...really."

"Why won't you tell me?"

"It doesn't matter—not yet anyway. I promise I'll tell you—soon."

"Why not now?"

"Please, Tommy."

"Whatever," I said, figuring if I had my secrets, she could have hers.

I kissed her gently on the lips, then I went to go pee.

Four

Sometimes when I woke up in the morning and saw a girl's face in my bed I panicked, wishing I'd talked her into going home the night before, but when I saw Janene sleeping next to me I felt like the luckiest guy in New York. Even without a stitch of makeup she was a knockout and I was glad just to be close to her. Maybe this was exactly what I needed in my life—stability, a nice, steady relationship.

I decided to wake her up in a special way. She was surprised at first, wiggling her legs, but then she relaxed and enjoyed herself. Afterwards, looking up at her, I said, "Sleep tight?"

"That was wonderful," she said, her face still red, trying to catch her breath.

She tried to take her turn, but I pulled her back up and said, "Nah, that's all right—that was a present for you. Actually, I was gonna ask you if you wanted some breakfast in bed. Want me to go out and get some bagels and coffee?"

"What time is it?"

I looked at the clock on the dresser.

"Five to seven."

"Shit—I have to be at work by a quarter to nine."

"Call in sick today."

"I wish I could, but my company's in the middle of

this important audit—my boss would kill me. Do you have a T-shirt or something I could put on?"

"Sure," I said. I went to the dresser and took out a Fruit of the Loom V-neck. She put on the T-shirt, pulling the covers up to hide her body, then she stood up out of bed. She was a big girl, but on her my T-shirt looked like a nightgown.

She went into the bathroom, taking her clothes with her. When I heard her put the toilet seat down I got up quickly and took my wallet out of the pocket of the jeans I was wearing last night and hid it in my dresser drawer under my socks. A few minutes later, Janene came out of the bathroom, fully dressed except for her shoes. I was back in bed in my underwear.

"I had a great time last night," she said.

"Me too."

"I wish I could spend the whole day with you."

"We'll have plenty of time for that," I said. I stood up and kissed her. "Can I walk you home?"

"You don't have to."

"I want to," I said. "The more time I get to spend with you the better."

I started getting dressed.

"So what are you gonna do today?" she asked.

"First, I have some shit to take care of around the building, then I have an audition to go to."

"An audition? You didn't tell me that."

"It's no big deal. It's to be in a dog food commercial."

"That sounds great."

"There's a lot of competition, but I think I have a good shot of getting it."

"Well, good luck."

"Do you have some money to lend me?"

I couldn't believe I said it like that—not even building up to it.

She looked at me for a second or two—it seemed longer—then said, "Sure…I guess so."

"Oh, didn't I tell you?" I said. "I think I lost my wallet yesterday."

"No, you *didn't* tell me that."

"Yeah, yesterday afternoon. I was doing some laundry and when I came back from the laundromat my wallet was gone. I looked all over my apartment for it, but I couldn't find it anywhere."

"That's awful."

"I probably dropped it on the street or maybe somebody picked my pocket. Anyway, it was no big deal really—I only had a few dollars in it and, luckily, I had my driver's license at home. I already called the bank and the credit card companies and they're gonna send me new cards. The bank's gonna Express Mail me a card this afternoon."

"So how much do you need?"

"I don't know. I guess fifty bucks should hold me over. It's just for today. If my boss was around this afternoon I'd—"

"It's no problem at all," she said. "The thing is, I only have about twenty dollars in my pocketbook. But if you wanted to walk out together we could pass a cash machine and I can—"

"I'd really appreciate that," I said. "I'll pay you back tomorrow. I'll come by your apartment if—"

"It's all right," she said. "You can pay me back whenever you want to."

We left my apartment and went down to the street, holding hands. It was another freezing day, but not as windy as yesterday. We talked about the weather and about how she loved skiing. I told her how I once modeled for a ski catalog, but how I'd only gone skiing once in my life, about five years ago, and how I wasn't very good. But I told her I'd love to go with her sometime.

We went up First Avenue to the Citibank cash machine on the corner of Sixty-eighth Street. She punched in the code and I stood behind her, memorizing the digits—4-7-6-6-3-4.

When she was about to type in the amount of money she wanted to withdraw I said, "You think you can make it a hundred instead of fifty? I mean if it's a problem forget about it, but I needed to buy some cleaning supplies for the building. If I don't clean today my landlord'll get pissed off. He has this bad Greek temper and I really don't feel like dealing with it."

"Sure," she said. "A hundred's no problem."

"Thanks," I said. "This is really nice of you."

I walked her to her building on York Avenue near Seventy-first Street. It was a pretty nice elevator building. I felt like shit for taking her back to my dump two dates in a row.

In front of the building we hugged and kissed.

"I had an amazing time last night," she said.

"Me too."

"So will I hear from you this time?"

She laughed, trying to make it into a joke, but I knew she was serious.

"You kidding?" I said. "I'm dying to go out with you again. How's tonight sound?"

"Tonight?"

"Yeah. How about you meet me at the bar around midnight? We can hang out awhile, then, if you're up for it, we can go out for a little bite. Maybe this time we'll make it to the restaurant."

We both laughed.

"Unless it's too soon," I said.

"No, it's not too soon."

"Wait, I forgot—you have to work tomorrow so maybe we should wait till Friday or Saturday."

"It's okay," she said. "I can make it tonight."

"You sure?"

"Positive. I'll see you at midnight."

We kissed and hugged for a while longer, then I walked away, looking back every few steps and waving. At the corner, I turned and I waved again.

I did some chores around the building—the guy in Apartment 2 had a leak in his radiator—then I cleaned the hallways and stairs, dumping out buckets of half water, half Clorox, and mopping up. My neighbors were mainly interns at New York Hospital and young college grads. They were nice enough people, but I kept to myself mostly, only talking to them if I had to do work in their apartments.

Around ten o'clock, I finished cleaning and went to

a deli on First Avenue and bought a couple of bacon-and-egg sandwiches. I started eating the sandwiches on my way home and finished them in my apartment. Then I started getting ready for the audition.

When I got out of the shower I put on the outfit my manager had told me to wear—jeans and a white V-neck T-shirt. In the commercial, I was going to play an average Joe, a working-class guy who lives alone with his dog. My manager thought it would be a good idea if I looked scruffy and a little tired so I didn't shave.

When I was dressed and ready to go, I practiced my one line in front of the mirror. I had to kneel down next to a dog and say, "He eats great and looks great, too." I practiced saying the line as many ways as I could think of, until I thought I had it down perfectly. They'd have to be crazy not to pick me.

The audition was at a studio on Fifty-seventh Street near Seventh Avenue. I took the 6 train downtown, switching for the R at Fifty-ninth. I arrived at twelve-thirty, a half hour before I had to go on.

As usual, there were dozens of guys in the waiting area who looked like they could be my twin brothers. They were all wearing white V-necks and hadn't shaved.

I was practicing the line in my head, still positive I was going to get the part. My turn came. I went into the room where the director, producer, and a few other guys—probably the writers and ad execs—were sitting behind a long desk. There was also a woman with curly brown hair, holding a golden retriever on a leash.

"Tommy Russo," the director said. He was a thin guy with short blond hair and glasses. He was wearing a black turtleneck.

"That's me," I said.

"Thank you for coming down," he said.

"My pleasure," I said.

"If you could just stand right over there," he said, pointing toward a piece of masking tape on the floor, about ten yards in front of the desk.

I went to the spot and the woman came toward me with the dog. But as soon as she tried to take off the leash, the dog started barking, going nuts. She tried to calm it down, saying "Easy" and "It's okay," but nothing helped.

"I'm sorry," the woman said to me. "She's usually not like this."

At first, the guys at the table were laughing, like they thought it was a big joke. But after a few minutes went by and the dog was still barking, trying to come after me, they started checking their watches and whispering to each other.

"Maybe you should take her out of here!" the director finally yelled to the woman so she could hear him over the crazy dog.

The woman started to walk away, but the dog kept pulling her back, scratching the floor, trying to come after me. Finally, the woman and the dog left the room, but I could still hear the dog barking somewhere.

"I guess I must've put on the dog-biscuit cologne this morning," I said. Nobody laughed.

"I'm very sorry about this," the director said.

"It's not your fault," I said. "I mean blame the dog, right?"

"We'll contact your manager or agent if any other roles come along."

I stood there for a couple of seconds before it set in, but then I still couldn't believe it.

"I don't get it," I said. "Don't you want to hear me read the line?"

"I don't think that'll be necessary," the director said.

Again I stared at him, then I said, "Why not?"

"Because you're not getting along with Molly."

"Who's Molly?"

"Molly is the dog."

"So bring Molly back in here. Maybe she'll calm down."

"I'm sorry, Mr. Russo, but we have to see the next actor now."

"I'm sorry, too," I said, "because I don't think this is fair. I came all the way down here, I practiced for this part. The least you could let me do—"

"Please leave, Mr. Russo."

"I just want to read my line," I said. "If you'd just sit back for a second you'd see—"

"I asked you nicely to leave, Mr. Russo. We're not hiring you for this role so you're just wasting all of our time by being here. So I'll ask you nicely one last time—please leave."

I knew the smart thing to do was to walk out of there, keep my mouth shut.

"Why do you think you can talk to people this way?" I said. "Just because you're a big shot, sitting over there behind your desk?"

The director whispered something to the guy next to him and the guy took out a cell phone and started making a call.

"If you want to avoid a very bad scene," the director said, "you'll turn around and leave right now."

"I'm not going anywhere," I said.

The director and the other guys were standing up now, talking to each other. I heard the director call me an "asshole" and something in me snapped. I went after him, climbing over the desk. He backed away and the other guys tried to hold me back. I broke free, then two security guards came up behind me and pulled me out of the room. They escorted me out of the building and said if I ever showed up there again I'd be arrested.

Walking along Fifty-seventh Street, I couldn't believe what had just happened. I knew if I thought about it anymore I'd really start getting down on myself, so I did what I always did when I wanted to take my mind off my problems—I stopped at a newsstand and bought the *Racing Form*, then I headed crosstown toward the OTB Inside Track on Second Avenue.

I hung out upstairs, at a table in the back under the sun roof. The usual degenerates were there—guys I saw all the time, but I didn't know any of their last names. A couple of people were my age, but almost everybody else was over sixty. Sometimes I got depressed, thinking about these guys who'd retired to spend more time with their wives and their kids, but they wound up spending all their time betting. I knew I wasn't as bad as they were, but I also knew I could wind up like them if I didn't watch out.

The third race was going off. I played the one and the horse jogged—suddenly, I was up over three hundred bucks. When I was collecting, I gave Lucy, the teller, a five-dollar tip. I didn't like anything in the fourth so I sat it out. But in the fifth I loved a horse. I was going to bet a hundred bucks, then I decided, what the hell, and I let the three hundred ride. The horse got caught in a speed duel and faded to last. By two o'clock, I was back home, broke again, watching TV.

Now all I could think about was the audition. Maybe if what happened today had happened a few years ago, or even a few months ago, things would've been different. I would've thanked the director for his time and walked calmly out of the building. But I guess there's a limit to how much abuse one man can take. After over thirteen years of trying to make it as an actor and not getting anywhere, it was hard to stay calm sometimes.

I decided to get back up on my horse—stop feeling sorry for myself.

I called my manager to see if he had any more auditions for me to go on. Danielle, his secretary, told me to hold on, then she came back and said Martin was out of the office.

"But I thought you said he was *in* the office," I said.

"I *thought* he was in the office," Danielle said, "but he wasn't at his desk."

I'd known Danielle a long time and I could tell she was lying.

"I know he's there," I said. "Could you please just tell him to take my call? I'll only take a minute, tops."

"Hold on a second," she said.

A minute or two went by, then Martin came on the line.

"So what's the deal," I said, "you don't want to take my phone calls?"

"I was going to call you later today anyway," Martin said.

"What's going on?" I said. "You got something hot for me to go on? Because if you do I'm ready to go. I'll even go out again today."

"I think we should end our relationship, Tommy."

"What?" I said, but I'd heard him loud and clear.

"I spoke with Kevin Parker and he told me what happened this afternoon at your audition."

"Oh, *that*," I said. "Look, I can explain—"

"I don't need an explanation. The fact is I think both of us know this isn't working out. We'd probably both be better off if you found somebody else to represent you."

"But I didn't do anything wrong," I said. "I just wanted to read my line and he wouldn't let me. I know it was wrong of me to open my mouth, but I couldn't help it. If you want me to call him up and apologize—"

"I don't think that'll be necessary, Tommy. Look, I know how badly you want to make it as an actor and

I'm not saying you should quit, but maybe you shouldn't approach it as seriously as you have been. In any case, I think a new manager can only help."

"But don't you even want to hear my side of the story?"

"It has nothing to do with what happened today—"

"Bullshit. If that asshole Kevin Parker didn't call you up you'd never be dumping me now."

"I'm sorry, Tommy, I have to go—"

"Please, Martin. I didn't mean…the guy was baiting me. He wanted me to blow up."

"I have to go. Goodbye, Tommy."

"Wait, don't—"

He hung up. I slammed the phone down. I sat calmly for a few seconds, then I yanked the cord out of the wall and tossed the phone across the room. Screaming, I kicked a chair out of my way, then I tore down the poster from *Raging Bull* and ripped it to shreds. I ripped up my head shot and picked up the phone and threw it across the room again. Finally, I sat down on the couch with my head in my hands.

For a while, I was mad at Martin. The fucking guy couldn't make it as an actor himself, so now he was taking it out on every other wannabe actor in the city. He was just like the directors and the producers— saying whatever he felt like saying because he knew he had the power to get away with it. But then, as I started to calm down, I decided it wasn't really Martin's fault. He'd been good to me over the years, probably sticking with me a lot longer than any other manager would have. Besides, he wasn't the one going to those auditions, getting turned down for role after role. I had nobody to blame for that but myself.

Martin was right—it was probably time for me to stop taking acting so seriously. It had nothing to do with talent because if you put me in auditions with other actors and all things were equal I knew I'd get the roles every time. But that was just it—all things *weren't* equal. To make it as an actor you had to be part of the clique. You had to go to one of the big-time acting schools—graduate from Yale or N.Y.U., or you had to have some famous teacher or acting coach— Meisner, Stani-fucking-slavsky. Those people were "in the business." But if you were like me, and you didn't have the fancy connections, you didn't have a shot in hell of making it.

I took my wallet from my jeans' pocket and slid out Pete Logan's business card which had Alan Schwartz's phone number on the back of it. I plugged the phone back into the wall—amazingly, it still worked—and dialed. On the second ring a snobby-sounding woman answered, "Alan Schwartz's office."

"Yeah, can I speak to Alan Schwartz?" I said.

"May I ask who's calling please?" she said, treating me like dirt.

"Tommy Russo."

"Is he expecting your call, Mr. Russo?"

"Yeah…I mean no…I mean kind of. Tell him Pete Logan said I should call him."

The line was dead, like she might have hung up, then she said, "Hold please," like it was busting her balls to transfer a call to her boss. Music came on—

Stevie Wonder singing "Part-Time Lover." Then the secretary came back on and said, "Mr. Schwartz is in a meeting now—he'll have to call you back."

"Shit," I said.

"Excuse me?"

"When's the meeting gonna be over?"

"He has meetings all afternoon. Would you like to leave a message or shall I connect you to his voice mail?"

"You think it'll be over soon?"

I heard her take a deep breath. "I'll connect you to his voice mail."

Before I could say anything else, I heard a click, then Alan Schwartz's voice came on.

This is the message I left:

"Hey, Alan, my name's Tommy—Tommy Russo. You don't know me, but a guy I think you know, said he was a good friend of yours, named Pete Logan, said I should throw you a call if I wanted to go in on that horse deal with you. Well, I want in, so can you give me a call when you have a chance? My home number's 646-879-4355. All right? Thanks a lot, Mr. Schwartz, I mean Alan. Take it easy."

As soon as I hung up I realized how stupid I was. First of all, I wasn't going to be home tonight. What if he called me back and I missed the call? Or what if he left a message and my answering machine was on the blink?

I called Pete at the Kings Highway branch of his shoe store. I didn't think he'd be there but I figured I could at least leave another message. A girl picked up and I asked for Pete. "Hold on," she said, then a guy came on the line and said, "This is Pete."

His voice didn't sound like it did at jai-alai. On the phone, he had a heavy Brooklyn accent.

"This Pete Logan?"

"Who's this?"

"This is Tommy Russo. You know, from jai-alai."

He didn't say anything for a couple of seconds, then he said, "Hey, how's it going? I didn't think I was gonna be hearing from you."

"Why not?"

"I don't know, it's just a surprise, that's all. So what's going on?"

"Not much," I said. "So you still need a fifth guy for that syndicate?"

"Far as I know."

"Then stop looking 'cause you found your man."

"You're kidding me?" he said. "That's terrific. So you…the money isn't a problem?"

"No problem at all."

"Great. You call Alan yet?"

"That's why I'm calling you. I left a message for him but I didn't want him to go out and find somebody else."

"You don't gotta worry about that. Alan would have to approve any new guy with the rest of us, so as soon as I hear from him I'll tell him we can stop our search. And we *can* stop it, right? I mean you're a hundred percent about this, right?"

"Yeah," I said. "I mean I want to meet with the

other guys first and see what it's all about. But if it all checks out…"

"I got you, I got you," Pete said. "This is great— exactly what I was hoping for when we started this thing—to get some real racing fans involved. There're a lot of guys who could put up the money, but what fun would that be? We want guys who love the sport, who always dreamed of owning a horse but never thought they'd be able to."

"That's me," I said, wondering how the hell I was going to come up with the ten grand.

Five

When I arrived at O'Reilley's at five-thirty, Gil, the regular day bartender, was behind the bar, reading a paperback. I asked him if Frank was around and he shook his head.

"But he's coming in today, right?"

"Yeah, he called before. He'll be in soon."

Gil went back to reading his book—*Resurrection* by Leo Tolstoy. Gil was about twenty-five and he had black curly hair and wore wire-rimmed glasses. Whenever he wasn't serving customers, he always seemed to be reading a book or writing in a pad. He said he wrote short stories and poems, but nobody in the bar had ever read anything he wrote. I used to think that the guy was doing the right thing—working at a bar to support his dream—but now I realized what a loser he was.

At six o'clock, Gil's shift was over and Gary wasn't in yet so I took over at the bar. Usually, Thursdays were good nights for happy hour, but maybe the cold was keeping people away because it was seven o'clock and there were only five people in the whole place— a couple of girls at the bar drinking screwdrivers, and a few guys in suits drinking beer, standing behind the girls, trying to get up the balls to go over and talk to them.

I put a CD—"The All-Time Best Party Songs"—into the stereo, then I leaned against the bar, flipping pages of the *Daily News* as Meat Loaf sang "Paradise By The Dashboard Light."

This was basically the way things were when Debbie O'Reilley came into the bar.

As usual, she was smashed. She could barely stand on her high heels and she had a big drunk smile. Her makeup was caked on and she was wearing long white shiny boots, a red miniskirt, and a short fur coat. Her fake D- or E-cup boobs were sticking straight out, pressing against her tight blouse. She looked like one of those cheap hookers on the West Side Highway, a hooker ten years past her prime.

I never really understood why Frank had married Debbie, but I figured it was because she was young and sexy—well, young as far as Frank was concerned —and I guess she *was* kind of sexy. She was an ex-table dancer, in one of those clubs the Mayor closed down on Seventh Avenue, and for a woman who must have been pushing fifty, she definitely had a nice shape. But a good body wasn't a reason to marry a woman and there wasn't much else to like about her. She was always nasty to Frank, especially when she was drunk, talking to his face about the other guys she was fucking, and Frank was rich as hell. He owned a bar and a big three-bedroom apartment on East Seventy-second Street. A lot of good-looking women would probably be clawing to meet a rich, successful guy like him, but instead he'd married a sleazy alcoholic who obviously didn't love him and who always treated him like dirt.

The only explanation I could come up with was that Frank was lonely. Frank's first wife had died a long time ago and maybe he just wanted somebody to come home to at night. Or, maybe he just liked the excitement of having a crazy alcoholic like Debbie in his life.

Debbie stopped in the middle of the room and looked around, staring at people the way drunks do. Her skin was dark brown and leathery. Finally, still wobbling, she said, "Where the hell is my husband?"

Normally, I tried not to talk too much to Debbie, especially when she was loaded. I knew she was just looking to start trouble and that if I just ignored her she'd go bother somebody else. But nobody else in the bar answered her so I said, "He's not here."

"Really?" She smiled, like I'd meant it as a joke. "Well where is he then?"

"Gil said he'd be in soon," I said.

"I guess my brilliant stepson isn't here either."

"Nah," I said.

"What was that?"

"He's not here," I said louder. I was still looking down at the newspaper.

"I'm sure he's out job-hunting," she said. She waited a second then said, "That was a joke—you can laugh, you know. Give me *some* hint that you're alive."

I didn't say anything.

"You're in a peachy mood tonight, aren't you?" she said. I was hoping she'd leave or go bother somebody else. Instead, she came up to the bar and sat down across from me. It smelled like she'd put on a whole bottle of perfume. She put her hand on top of mine and said, "Gimme something stiff."

Debbie was always coming on to me, just like she came on to practically any other guy with a pulse when she was drunk.

But, for some reason, I didn't move my hand away.

I said, "You really think you should be drinking any more?"

"What are you talking about?" she said. "I haven't had a drink all day."

"Yeah right. If you weren't wearing all that perfume I bet I'd be able to smell the booze on your breath."

"You know," she said in a quieter, sexier voice, "if you want to get a closer whiff you can."

Now I moved my hand.

"If you want something make it yourself," I said. I took my newspaper and walked to the other end of the bar.

"That's no way to treat your boss's wife," she said. "You realize your job could be on the line for this kind of behavior."

I asked the two girls if they were okay with their screwdrivers. One of them asked for a refill. I made the drink, got her change, thanked her for the buck tip, then went back to reading the newspaper. Debbie stood there for a while, staring at me, then she sat down on the stool next to the blonde. The Meat Loaf song ended and now The Romantics were singing, "What I Like About You."

"I'm still waiting for my drink," Debbie said.

"The bar's all yours," I said. "Want a drink, make one."

"All right," Debbie said. "I think I will."

She came behind the bar and made herself a drink. I wasn't watching, but I knew she was making her usual Scotch and soda. I started talking to the two girls. Then Debbie came and brushed up against me. She interlocked her arm around mine and said to the two girls, "Sorry, he's coming home with me tonight."

"Don't pay any attention to her," I said.

"What?" Debbie said. "You forgot about our date tonight? Shame on you."

Usually, I didn't care what Debbie said to me, figuring she was just a drunk who didn't know any better, but with the girls there I felt like I had to say something.

"Why don't you just get the hell out of here?"

"I will," she said, "if you come with me." She pinched my ass.

"I'm serious," I said, wanting to hit her. "Just get the hell out of here."

"I love angry men."

She tried to pinch me again. This time I grabbed her wrist before she could squeeze.

"Let go of me."

"I told you to leave me alone."

"Let go!"

"You gonna leave me alone?"

"Just let go!"

Her face was turning red. I let go.

Rubbing her arm, she said, "If I tell Frank about

this you know what'll happen, don't you? You'll get fired. You'll be out on the street."

I tried not to look at her. The whole thing was so stupid—she was out-of-her-mind drunk and even if she did tell Frank on me I knew he wouldn't care. He'd probably done the same thing to her hundreds of times, or at least he'd thought about doing it.

Debbie stood facing me for a few seconds, shifting her eyes with the dark blue eye shadow all around them, back and forth, then she stormed away, taking her drink with her, of course. She sat down in her original seat at the other end of the bar. I apologized to the two girls for the "disturbance," but they seemed freaked out about the whole thing.

The girls stood up and put on their coats. As they were leaving, Frank walked in. Wearing a long beige trench coat and carrying two shopping bags, he looked like a tired old man. He was old, I guess, but not very old. He'd celebrated his sixty-fifth birthday last year, but he looked more like seventy. He was short, stocky, and he combed long gray hairs from the back and sides of his head to cover a big bald spot in the middle.

"There he is," Debbie said, "my handsome, hardworking, sexy, irresistible, loser of a husband."

Debbie continued to insult Frank and then she asked him for money—a hundred dollars. Frank said, "I'm not giving you any more money to get drunk with," and then Debbie started yelling at him—cursing and calling him all kinds of names. As usual, Frank just took the abuse like a wimp. With everybody else, Frank was a take-charge guy, but he could never stand up to his wife. It was like Debbie had some weird power over him—he was Superman and she was made out of kryptonite. Whenever she was clawing over some guy or making a drunken fool out of herself he'd just ignore it, like it didn't mean anything to him. Whenever I tried to talk to him about it—figuring the guy always helped me out, the least I could do was try and help him—he'd always just say "Forget about it" or "Who cares?" I never pushed him, figuring there are some things guys just need to keep to themselves.

"You're a fucking asshole!" Debbie yelled. "You're pathetic! Look at those clothes you're wearing, like it's 1972! When was the last time you went shopping? Face it, you're an antique, a dinosaur, a pathetic time capsule of a man. I'm ashamed to be your wife!"

A few more customers—a group of guys in hockey jerseys, probably here to watch the Devil game later on—came into the bar. I asked them what they wanted, but when they saw Debbie yelling at Frank like a lunatic they put their coats back on and left.

Debbie had cost Frank a ton of business over the past few years.

Finally, Debbie put her own coat on, getting ready to leave.

"Maybe you'd like to know the name of the guy I'm fucking tonight," she yelled at Frank's back as he walked away toward the kitchen. "His name's Jean-Claude. He's French or Canadian or French-Canadian—whatever. Anyway, from what I understand he has a very big cock. Much bigger than yours anyway, although a five-year-old boy has a bigger cock than you!"

A couple of guys standing near Debbie started to laugh. I wanted to laugh too, because it was kind of funny, but out of respect for Frank I held back. Frank just shook his head, continuing to the back of the bar.

Debbie came over to me and said, "I'm sorry. It was wrong of me to grab you like that."

"Forget about it," I said.

"I was watching you," she said, slurring her words, "talking to those two girls. You know my offer still stands."

I knew what her "offer" was. She was always inviting me to "stop by" at her apartment some afternoon when Frank wasn't around for "a good time." She was smiling, running her tongue across her upper lip. I noticed the way some of her lipstick had come off on her shiny capped teeth. I could also see some of her fake cleavage popping out of her black-and-gold blouse. I had to admit, for an old lady there was definitely something sexy about her. If she wasn't Frank's wife, I might've even thought about taking her up on her offer.

"You better get going," I said. "You don't wanna keep your French boy waiting."

At seven-thirty, Gary finally showed up and took over for me at the bar. I ate a burger and some fries in the kitchen, then I knocked on the door to Frank's office.

"Come in," he said.

He was sitting at his desk, looking up at me over his reading glasses.

"Oh, it's you," he said. "I thought it might be my delightful wife."

"You got a second?"

"Sure. Sit down."

I sat in a chair across from him. The office was a mess with file folders, newspapers and magazines piled up everywhere. Frank put down the papers he'd been reading and said, "What am I gonna do with her, Tommy?"

"That's up to you," I said. "You already know what I think."

"It's never been as bad as it is now," he said. "Every night she's like this. I try to reason with her—get her to go to A. A. or see a shrink—but she just doesn't think she has a problem."

"That's because she *is* the problem."

"You're right—I know you're right—believe me. You know she's placing ads in newspapers now? I heard her on the phone calling one of the neighborhood papers, I think it was *Our Town*. She was reading the ad to them over the phone: 'Lonely married woman looking for a good time and more.' Then, last week, I come home early from work and she has a guy over at the apartment—*our* apartment. I can hear them going at it from the living room, so I go bang on the bedroom door, thinking I'm gonna kill whoever she's in there with. Then the bedroom door opens and this big black guy—seven feet tall, like a basketball player—comes out."

"Maybe it *was* a basketball player," I said. "I hear those guys get around."

Frank shot a look at me.

"I didn't mean it like that," I said. "I was just trying—"

"I know," Frank said. "If I were you I'd think I was a pathetic joke too."

"I don't think *that*."

"I know it's hard for you to believe," he said, "because you didn't know her until a couple years ago, but she used to be so much different. She was a warm, friendly, outgoing, generous woman. Then she started hitting the bottle and—well, you've seen her. I keep telling myself that it can't possibly get any worse, she's definitely hit rock-bottom this time, then she's putting ads in the paper and sleeping with men right under my nose."

"You must like it," I said

"What do you mean? I hate it!"

"That's what you *say*—but if you really hated it you would've kicked her out the first time she cheated on you, like any normal guy would've. But since you're staying with her, hoping that she'll change, you obviously like the abuse."

"Never mind."

"See—that's what you always say when you know I'm right, 'Never mind.' Well, if you really knew I was right you wouldn't just sit there. You'd do something about it."

"What about you?" Frank said, trying to change the subject.

"What about me?"

"How's everything in your life going?"

"Not bad," I said.

"Yeah? How's the acting coming along?"

"Pretty good."

"Really? I haven't heard you talking about it for a long time. I hope you're still taking it seriously."

"I am."

"Good. I'm glad. You know how much confidence I have in you, Tommy. I'm still waiting for you to come in here one day and tell me that you're quitting your job—that you're going out to Hollywood. Remember—all I want is a front-row seat at the premiere of your first movie."

"You never know," I said, remembering how I was thrown out of the audition this afternoon.

"So did you come in here to talk about anything else?" Frank asked. "I have to finish looking over these books and then I have to go out and take care of a few things."

"Actually, I was having a little problem and I thought you could help me out."

"Help you out with what?" Frank said, like he knew what was coming.

"I know I'm a few weeks ahead on my salary already, but I was hoping you could, you know—shoot me a little advance."

Frank was glaring at me.

"Are you gambling again?"

I was ready to say no—make up some story—but I couldn't bullshit Frank. The guy had been like a father to me—the father I'd always wished I'd had.

"A little bit," I said.

"How much is a little bit?"

"I just need a few hundred bucks," I said, "for rent and bills and—"

"What are you trying to do," Frank said, "screw up your life? Why are you wasting your time gambling? You're how old now, thirty-two, thirty-three? This is the time you should be going all-out, trying to make it with your acting."

"Look, I don't need the speech, all right—"

"Then what will it take to get through to you? You always tell me you're through gambling, you're gonna give it up—"

"I have it under control."

"Under control? Meanwhile, you keep blowing your money at the track, coming to me for advances, and you think you have it under control? How much money are you into me for? A thousand, two thousand? You're a compulsive gambler, Tommy. You have a sickness—like drinking, like anything else."

I stood up and said, "Look, if you don't want to give me the money you don't have to."

"You have to learn your lesson eventually. Maybe this'll be your wake-up call. Maybe you'll start going to G.A. like you should've months ago. I'm sorry, but I'm not going to bail you out this time."

"Fine," I said.

"I'm doing this for your own good Tommy. You know how much I care about you. Maybe now you won't throw your life away."

I left Frank's office and went to the bar. I poured myself a pint of Sam Adams. I was pissed off at Frank for being so tough on me when he was so soft on his wife, but I knew he was right about one thing—gambling wasn't the answer. Whenever I was at the track or the OTB, around all those degenerates, I always felt like the world's biggest loser.

But the only way to make money fast was to win it and I knew I could win ten grand. I just needed a stake to bet with and then I had to get on a little hot streak. My only problem was getting the stake.

It was a slow night at the door which gave me a lot of time to think.

At midnight, Janene showed up. Until I saw her walk into the bar I'd completely forgotten about our date tonight.

"You look great," I said, and it was true. She was wearing tight jeans and a tight purple velvet top.

"Thanks," she said. "So do you."

We hung out by the door, talking. She asked me how my audition went and I said, "Okay." She said she hoped I got the part and I said, "I wouldn't bet on it." I got off work early, around one-thirty, and Janene and I left the bar together.

"So do you want to go to a diner or something?" I asked.

"Are you hungry?"

"Not really, but I can always eat."

"If you want we can just go back to my place—you know, to hang out and talk."

Janene had had a couple of drinks at the bar and she seemed a little drunk.

"You sure you want to do that?" I said. "I mean I

remember what you said last night about taking it too fast."

"I was just being insecure," she said, grabbing my hand and squeezing it. "Don't pay any attention to me."

We walked toward her apartment, holding hands, stopping every once in a while to make out.

Her apartment was on the sixth floor at the end of a long hallway. It was a big one-bedroom, at least twice the size of my dump. There was even a living room with a white couch, a coffee table, a rug, and some other expensive-looking furniture.

As soon we got inside and Janene turned on the light, I came up behind her, putting my hands around her waist, and started kissing the back of her neck and under her jaw. She stood there for a while, letting me go on, then she moved away.

"What's wrong?" I asked.

"Nothing," she said. "It's just...don't you want to come inside for a tour first?"

"I figured you could give me the tour in the morning."

I tried to put my arms around her again but she pushed me back and said, "I'm serious."

She walked away into the living room.

"What's the matter?" I said. "Did I do something wrong?"

"No," she said. "It's just...I don't know...Forget it."

"Hey, if you don't feel comfortable with me here it's no problem. I'd be happy to—"

"No, that's not it," she said. "Of course I want you

to be here. It's just, I was hoping we could sit down for a while, and talk and…I really have to go to the bathroom."

"Are you sure nothing's wrong?"

"No. Please. I'm sorry."

I waited on the couch while she went into the bathroom. She was taking a long time. I wondered what I could have said or done to piss her off. There was a copy of *House Beautiful* on the coffee table and I started looking through it. Finally, she came out and said, "You want some tea?"

"I don't drink tea," I said.

"You want something else to drink? Coke, 7UP, water…?"

"I'm all right," I said.

She turned on the stove, putting up water for tea, then she came back into the living room and sat next to me on the couch.

"I'm sorry for the way I've been acting," she said. "Really, you didn't do anything wrong. It's not you, it's me. It's just…"

"What? Come on, you can tell me."

My hand was on her thigh.

"Well, it's this, what you're doing now—holding my hand. Touching me. Why weren't you like this before at the bar?"

"What do you mean?"

"I tried to hold your hand a couple of times, but you kept pulling away. I was just wondering—are you embarrassed about me or something?"

I laughed.

"What's so funny?"

"That's a good one," I said. "Embarrassed to be with a beautiful woman like you."

"Well, that's how it *seemed*."

"I was proud to be with you," I said. "I wanted to be all over you at the bar, but I didn't know if you wanted me to. I mean I remembered what you'd said last night about how we might be going too fast and—"

"Are you being honest with me?"

"Of course I am. What are you talking about?"

"Never mind," she said. "I told you I was the one with the problem, not you."

We started making out. She had her hand on my leg when she said, "So you got a new wallet, huh?"

At first I had no idea what she was talking about. Luckily, I caught on fast.

"No, that's the old one. I found it in my apartment. It turned out I didn't lose it after all."

"Well, *that* must've been a relief."

"Shit," I said. "I didn't have a chance to hit the bank before work to take your money out. But I could go out right now if you want me to?"

"No, it's okay," she said.

"You sure?" I said, knowing there was no way she'd send me out into the cold. "There's an ATM a few blocks away, right?"

"Don't be crazy, it's freezing out," she said. "Give it to me the next time we see each other or whenever. It's no big deal."

"I'm really sorry," I said.

We started to make out again, then she was lying on

the couch on her back and I was on top of her. I pulled back and smiled, looking into her eyes. Then, suddenly, something was different about her and I couldn't figure out what it was.

"What's the matter?" she asked.

For a few more seconds I stared at her, then it hit me.

"What happened to your eyes?"

"My eyes?" she said, like she had no idea what I was talking about. "What do you mean?"

"They used to be blue."

"Oh, I didn't tell you about that?" she said. "I wear color contacts. They were itching me so I took them out."

"You mean your eyes aren't blue?"

"What's the matter? You don't like my eyes?"

"No, I like your eyes a lot," I said. "I just thought they were blue, that's all."

The tea kettle started to whistle. Janene went to the kitchen and came back with a mug of tea. She took a sip then put the mug down on the coffee table.

"There's something I need to talk to you about, Tommy."

"Shoot," I said.

"Well, remember last night, when I told you I had something important I wanted to tell you."

"Yeah."

"Well, I decided I want to tell you…tonight…right now."

"So go ahead and tell me."

"First you have to promise you won't be mad at me.

I mean it's not a big deal, but you might be mad that I didn't tell you."

"There's no way I could ever be mad at you."

"Okay, well…" She was looking down. "See, there's something about me you don't know. It's just…you see—God, I don't know why this is so hard. I guess I might as well just say it—I'm married. Not really *married*—separated. I've been separated for over a year but, technically, I'm still married. I wanted to tell you the night we met, and then the first time we went out, but I didn't know how to bring it up."

"Wow," I said. "That's pretty heavy."

"I'm sorry I didn't tell you right away," she said. "I would've told you but—"

"It's all right," I said. "I mean it's not your fault."

"You're probably really mad at me now."

"Why would I be mad at you? So you're married. It's no big deal. So who's the lucky guy?"

"His name's Joe. I went to college with him at Stony Brook. We were only married two years and we were never really right for each other."

"That's cool," I said.

Her face brightened.

"You mean it?"

"Yeah," I said. "I mean it's not like you're living with him anymore or anything. And it's over, right?"

"Of course it's over. The divorce should come through in the next month or two—we've both been seeing other people. You're really not upset?"

"Why would I be upset?"

"You can't believe what a relief this is. I was obsessing

about it all day. I was afraid you'd freak out, that you'd
…I don't know…want to make a big deal out of it."

"I'm just happy to be with you tonight, that's all,"
I said.

We stayed on the couch for a while, making out,
and then we went into the bedroom.

She moved closer to me. Her head was wedged
between my arm and my chest. We were naked and
sweaty.

"It feels so nice to be with you," she said.

A few minutes later she was fast asleep.

I noticed the jewelry box on the dresser. I got out of
bed and dressed quietly. The light on the night table
was still on. In the dim yellow light I saw Janene still
facing the other way. A necklace and a bracelet were
out next to the jewelry box, but she'd probably notice
if they were missing. Instead, I reached inside the box
and took out a gold necklace, some diamond earrings,
and a gold bracelet. I put the jewelry in my pocket. In
the mirror above the dresser I saw that Janene was still
fast asleep. I tiptoed out of the room and left the
apartment.

Six

The next morning I drove to Chinatown. It wasn't hard finding a pawn shop down there—the hard part was finding a Chinese guy who spoke English. After walking in and out of a couple of places, I finally found an old guy who seemed to understand me at a place on Hester Street, off the Bowery. I cut a deal with him—he'd give me three hundred bucks for the jewelry and I could buy it back for three-fifty. He originally wanted to give me four hundred, but we made it three if he wouldn't put the stuff out for sale until tomorrow. The place closed at eight o'clock so I'd have plenty of time to buy the jewelry back before I went to work. Then I'd call Janene, figure out some way to explain why I took off last night, and find a chance to slip the jewelry back into her jewelry box.

From the Bowery, I hopped on the Manhattan Bridge to the BQE and about forty-five minutes later I was in the Aqueduct Racetrack parking lot in Ozone Park, Queens, sitting in my car, waiting for the gates to open. Leaving my apartment building this morning, I'd picked up a copy of the *Racing Form* and today nobody came over to bother me. I handicapped the whole card, letting the motor run to keep the inside of the car warm.

Walking into the track, I felt lucky.

I took the escalator up to the third floor. I once hit an exacta on the third floor for two Gs so I knew I had a much better chance of winning up there than on the first or second floors.

I won four hundred-plus dollars on the first race. I hit the second race *and* the daily double. Suddenly, I was up over a G. I lost the third race, hit the fourth and fifth, lost the sixth, and hit the seventh. I didn't like anything in the later races so I left the track with a little over three grand in my wallet.

It was a great ride back to the city—blasting The Stones and The Who, banging out the beat on the dashboard.

Now I only needed seven grand to join the syndicate. *Seven grand.* I could make that in one or two more bets. I just had to be patient—wait for my spot. The key was I couldn't just start betting wildly—I had to use my head. Over the next week I'd find a couple of solid bets—sure things. If I doubled my money two times that would give me more than enough to join.

It was a little after four o'clock when I crossed the Manhattan Bridge and arrived in Chinatown. The neighborhood was still packed with shoppers, but I found a parking spot right away, across the street from the pawn shop, proving that things were definitely going my way.

The old man was busy helping another customer so I hung out, looking at some Swiss Army knives in a display case. When the customer left I told the old man I was ready to buy back my jewelry.

I knew something was wrong when he acted like he couldn't speak English.

"Look," I said as slowly as I could. "I want my jewelry. Jew-el-ry. Can you un-der-stand what I'm say-ing?"

"Sorry, no jury," he said. "Jury sold. Sorry, you leave."

"Sold?" I said. "I think you must be making a mistake. I was the guy in here this morning—"

"No mistake," he said. "Jury sold. You leave."

"I don't understand," I said. "Don't you remember me?"

The old man yelled something in Chinese.

"What's wrong with you?" I said. "Why're you yelling? I just want to know where my jewelry is."

"What's going on here?"

I looked over my shoulder and saw a young Chinese guy pointing a gun at my face. I didn't know much about guns, but this one was big and silver and it looked like it could put a very big hole in my head.

"There seems to be a little misunderstanding here," I said. "See, I dropped off some jewelry here this morning—"

"We sold your jewelry to some lady," the young guy said.

"Why'd you do that?" I said. "Your boss promised me he wasn't gonna sell it."

"Well, he did. So why don't you just get the hell out of our store before I call the cops or shoot you. You decide which."

I stood there for a few seconds thinking, then I walked out. I kicked the side of my car as hard as I could, adding a new dent. I thought about hanging

out until the kid went home, then going back into the
store to talk to the old man again, but what good would
that do? It wouldn't get me Janene's jewelry back.

I still had over an hour before I had to be at work
so I went downtown to the OTB Teletheater on Water
Street.

The Aqueduct card was over so they were showing
races from Hollywood Park. It had to be an omen—
the place I was going to wind up someday as a horse
owner was on the TV screen. I bought a program.
There was a horse going off at three to one, and it
looked unbeatable. This was it, the spot I'd been waiting
for. I bet the whole three grand, figuring when it won
I'd get back twelve.

The race went off and I thought I must've bet on
the wrong horse. The horse I bet on always went to the
lead, but this pig was dead last. Then the announcer
said that the jockey had pulled my horse up on the
backstretch.

I couldn't believe it—I was broke again. The money
didn't even have a chance to get warm in my wallet.

When I got to work I was still numb. I had no idea
what I'd say when Janene came asking about her jewelry.

I poured a Sam Adams and sat at the bar. Jerry, one
of the old cronies who came to O'Reilley's every afternoon, was sitting next to me. He reeked of alcohol so I
knew he was lit.

"Hey, Tommy," he slurred, just noticing me next to
him, even though I'd been sitting there a couple of
minutes already. "How's it goin'?"

The last thing I was in the mood for was to get into

a conversation with some old drunk. I just nodded, staring straight ahead.

"I'm doin' all right," he said. "Seen better days, but who hasn't? I guess that's what getting older's all about. But I can't complain. I'm not dead—that's one good thing."

I didn't say anything. I was still thinking about that race at Hollywood Park and how I had screwed everything up. Then Jerry said "So did you buy your box yet for the Super Bowl pool?" and I said to myself: the Super Bowl pool. Of course, the Super Bowl pool.

Seven

Every year O'Reilley's had a Super Bowl pool. It was the same type of pool that just about every other bar in the city had. There were two columns of numbers, 0-9—one column for the AFC team, one column for the NFC team. For X number of dollars you got a box with two numbers that had to match the last digits of the score at the end of a quarter or, for the big prize, the end of the game. At O'Reilley's, boxes went for five hundred bucks apiece so the total prize money would be fifty thousand dollars. The Super Bowl was still over a month away, but at least half the boxes were already full. Frank was putting the money in the bank as it came in, but a bunch of guys bought boxes last week and the money was in the safe—and the safe was right behind the bar.

As Jerry went on, talking about whatever, I was thinking about a robbery. Getting in would be easy, the only question was when I would do it. From watching Frank over the years I already knew the combination by heart. It was a good thing I always noticed things like that. I'd only seen Janene punch the code of her ATM card into the machine that one time and I still had the digits memorized.

The best time to do it would be late at night, just before closing time. It would be the only time I could do it because there were always people around the bar at other times and I didn't have a key to the bar to come and go in the middle of the night. When I had the chance, I'd have to move fast. I couldn't put it off much longer either. I saw Frank going into the safe a few nights ago and saw those stacks of bills, but it was only a matter of time until he moved the cash to the bank, if he hadn't done it already.

The only thing that bothered me about my plan was that I'd be stealing from Frank. I knew he wouldn't suspect me—he liked me too much to think I'd ever do something like that to him. Chances were, he'd blame Debbie or Gary—probably Debbie. But he was the only person in the world who'd always been there for me when I needed him and I really didn't want to screw him over like that.

I went to the pay phone in the back of the bar and called home for my messages. There was one message:

"Hello, this is a message for Tommy Russo—Tommy, there was a very long beep on your machine so I hope you get this. This is Alan Schwartz, returning your call. So I hear you want to get involved in our little syndicate? Terrific. I don't know how much Pete told you, but if you leave your address with my secretary I'll FedEx you a copy of the contract we worked out. If you have any questions I'd be delighted to answer them. Unfortunately, I'll be out of the office most of the day today. Maybe we could all get together early next week sometime and discuss a strategy, etcetera, okay? Oh, and you can

give us your check then too. Okay? So let's talk for sure next week and I hope you have a good weekend. Goodbye, Tommy."

I hung up without saving the message. By eight o'clock there was already a nice-sized Friday night crowd in the bar and I was standing at the door proofing. I was in a good mood—laughing, joking around with everybody. I was even nice to Gary. When he showed up I said, "Hey, what's going on?" when I usually didn't say jack shit to him. He noticed the change in me and said, "You sure you're feeling all right tonight?"

"Never felt better in my life, buddy," I said.

After a while the crowd started to thin out and then Susan Lepidus showed up at the bar. She used to hang out at O'Reilley's a lot, then, about a year ago, we went out one night to a club on the West Side. I hadn't seen her in at least six months. She had curly red hair that went halfway down her back and she had a small, pretty face. She was with a short, dark-haired guy I'd never seen before.

"Hi, Tommy," she said, giving me a big warm smile.

"Haven't seen you in a while, huh?" I said.

"Maybe I've been hiding from you," she said.

"Well, I found you," I said.

We both laughed. Her boyfriend, watching us, didn't crack a smile.

"Tommy, I'd like you to meet Jim. Jim, this is Tommy."

I shook Jim's hand. He had a strong grip, the typical little guy trying to act tough.

I looked back at Susan and I thought I caught her staring at me.

"Anyway, we better get inside, it's freezing out here," she said. "I'll talk to you later, okay?"

"Okay," I said.

Susan and Jim went into the bar. Then, about a minute or two later, I was checking a few more IDs when I felt somebody touching my arm. I turned around and Susan was standing there.

"So how *are* you?" she said.

"Pretty good," I said. "So you don't come around here too much any more, huh?"

"I haven't been going out as much as I used to," she said. "I guess I'm getting boring in my old age."

"You don't look so boring to me." I said.

We both smiled. Her lips, coated with bright red lipstick, looked good.

"I better go," she said. "My friend's gonna be back from the bathroom in a second. But, you know, we should really go out again sometime. Why don't you give me a call?"

"I will," I said.

I watched Susan walk back to the bar. When Jim was facing the other way, ordering drinks, Susan looked back at me and smiled and waved.

When I first started working at O'Reilley's, I used to give Susan and her friends free drinks and Jello shots whenever I was bartending. I liked Susan a lot, but after that one date I'd never called her again. I guess it was the story of my life—when I had a good thing going I always found a way to screw it up.

But now I had a second chance. I wouldn't even have to ask her for her phone number because I still had it memorized.

Susan and Jim left around eleven—Susan touched my arm and kissed me on the cheek again on her way out—and the next time I looked at my watch it was after midnight. But there was still a pretty big crowd at the door and a lot of ID checking to do. Tonight would be a late night—last call wouldn't be until two-thirty. I was planning to make my move for the safe at around three, when the place was empty. I was usually alone in the bar for a little while after Gary went home and I was stacking chairs and stools.

"Tommy."

Her voice jolted me. The last person I wanted to see tonight was Janene. I was hoping she wouldn't discover her jewelry missing for a few days—that I'd have time to think up an excuse. She was standing at the front of the line of people waiting to get into the bar.

"Hey, how's it goin'?" I said, trying to act like I was happy to see her and nothing was wrong.

"I need to talk to you right away," she said.

She didn't dress up tonight. She was wearing sweatpants, a down winter coat, red earmuffs, and no makeup. Her eyes were blue again.

"All right," I said, "but it's gonna have to wait a few minutes. As you can see I'm checking IDs here."

"Did you steal my jewelry?"

"What?" I said, like I had no idea what she was talking about.

People on line were staring at us.

"It was a simple question. If you have my jewelry just give it back to me now and I won't call the police."

I laughed, shaking my head.

"Just relax, okay? Let me get these people into the bar, then I'll be right with you."

I checked IDs while Janene stood next to me, her arms crossed in front of her chest. I was glad to have the break—it gave me time to think about what I was going to say.

When the last person went into the bar, Janene said, "Well?"

"Well what?"

"Can I have my jewelry back please?"

"First of all, please don't ever come here while I'm working and pull a scene like this again. It's bad for business and I'll lose my job."

"Some job," she said, rolling her eyes. I had never hit a woman before in my life, but I wanted to hit Janene, slap her right across the face. I might've done it too, but we were on the street and people were watching.

"Second of all," I said, "I don't know what the fuck you're talking about. Jewelry? What jewelry?"

"You know what jewelry."

"Is this because I took off last night? Because if it is, I think you got the wrong idea."

"Look, I'm not an idiot, okay? I just want my jewelry back."

"I don't know what you're talking about and if you won't tell me I guess I'll never know."

I stared at her for a few seconds without blinking.

My acting experience was paying off. I was staying cool and relaxed and I could tell she was starting to believe me.

A couple of guys came up to the door. They looked over twenty-one so I just waved them in.

Janene said, "A necklace and my diamond studs are missing from my jewelry box."

So she didn't know about the bracelet. I'd have to remember not to say anything about that.

"So let me get this straight," I said. "You think I robbed you last night?"

"Did you?"

"Jesus Christ, what kind of guy do you think I am?"

"Then where's my jewelry?"

"How the hell should I know?"

She took a deep breath, then said, "All I know is I woke up in the middle of the night and you were gone. Then I came home from work today and noticed the stuff missing."

"So what makes you think I took it? Maybe somebody broke into your apartment this afternoon. Or maybe you were robbed a few days ago or a few months ago."

"I just wore those earrings last week."

"So somebody could've robbed you any day last week or this week. Why do you think I did it?"

This got her thinking. She looked at me closely, trying to see if I'd crack. I didn't.

She said, "If you were me, what would you think?"

"I'd think maybe it was an inside job. I knew a girl who lived in one of those elevator buildings and people were getting robbed all the time. D'you keep a key with your super?"

"Yeah, but he's a nice guy. He'd never rob me."

"And what, I'm not a nice a guy? Look, call the cops, do what you want. I don't have to take this."

I got up off my stool and started into the bar.

"Tommy."

I turned around slowly. I felt like I was in a play or a movie.

Janene said, "I'm sorry, all right? I just didn't know what to think. I mean after…why did you leave anyway? How could you do something like that to me?"

She was starting to cry. I stared at her for a few seconds, then said, "You didn't tell me about your husband. It didn't bother me at first, but then I thought about it some more and it did. I was very hurt."

"*You* were hurt?"

"Yeah. I felt like I wasn't important to you, like you were just rebounding with me, using me to get over your marriage."

"That's crazy."

"Is it?"

She stared at me. Obviously, I'd hit home.

"See?" I said. "It wasn't gonna work out anyway with us so what difference does it make?"

I started to walk away again when she said, "Tommy."

I stopped without turning around.

She said, "I'm sorry for everything."

"Forget about it," I said, walking into the bar. "It's too late."

*

The lights flashed for last call. There were a bunch of drunk guys, drinking pitchers of Bud, and I sped them along, telling them they had five minutes to finish their beer.

Gary was still behind the bar, cleaning up. Sometimes he was the last one to leave and I couldn't let that happen tonight.

"It's all right," I said. "I'll clean up for you."

He looked at me like he was surprised that I was talking to him.

"What did you do," he said, "take some happy pills before you came to work tonight?"

"Nah," I said, "I'm just in a good mood. Something wrong with that?"

"No, that's cool. I wanted to head downtown to hear this band play tonight anyway."

"Have fun."

"You sure you don't mind?"

"Forget about it," I said.

"That's really cool of you, man. I owe you one."

Gary finished what he was doing, then he went to the back to get his coat. Now all I had to do was clear out all the customers and I could get to work.

"All right," I said to the guys drinking pitchers, "it's time to call it a night."

"But we just got this pitcher," one of the guys said.

"Sorry, we're closing up right now," I said.

The guys chugged their beer then put on their coats and left.

A few minutes later, Gary said "See ya" and he left too. I went and locked the door behind him. Kathy and the busboys had gone home already, but Frank was still somewhere in the bar, probably working on the books in his back office. There were also still some guys in the kitchen. But at least the whole front of the bar was empty and I didn't know if I'd have a chance like this again.

I went behind the bar and got down on my knees. I knew the combination by heart and I knew it would only take me a few seconds to open the safe.

I fucked up the combination the first time and I had to do it again. I felt the veins in my forehead pulsing and sweat was dripping down the back of my neck. The safe didn't open the second time either. Maybe I was screwing up the numbers. Then, on the third try, I heard a click. The door swung open.

Seeing the money gave me a head rush. I had no idea how much was there, but there were stacks of fifties, twenties, and tens—mostly twenties—wrapped in rubber bands. I grabbed a stack of twenties, but realized I had no place to put it. Fuck, I didn't think about that. The pockets of my jeans were too tight and there were no bags lying around. Then I heard a sound—footsteps coming toward the front of the bar. I put the twenties back in the safe and shut the door quietly. The person was in the room now. I crawled to the other end of the bar so I'd be away from the safe and I stood up.

"Jesus Christ," Frank said, taking a few steps backwards. He was breathing hard. "You just scared the living shit out of me."

"I was just putting some bottles in the fridge," I said.

"Well don't pop up like that. Jesus."

"Sorry," I said.

"Eh, it's all right. Actually, I'm glad you're still here. You want to go get some breakfast with me?"

"I was just gonna head home," I said. "I mean after I finish up here."

"Where's Gary?"

"Went downtown to catch a band."

Frank rolled his eyes. "Come on, we'll finish that up tomorrow when we open. I really wish you'd just come out with me. I'm losing my mind and I need somebody to talk to. Food's on me."

I couldn't rob the safe tonight anyway—not after Frank saw me crawling around behind the bar—so I told him I'd go. I went to the back to wash up and get my jacket. I couldn't believe I didn't have that money. I could still feel the stack of bills in my hand and I could still see Andrew Jackson's face on the twenties. Some banks were open on Saturdays—maybe Frank was going to make a deposit tomorrow morning. This might've been my one shot at getting the money and I blew it.

We took a cab to the Green Kitchen on the corner of Seventy-seventh and First. Frank once told me how he'd been going there for twenty years and how it was his favorite diner in New York. As usual on a weekend night, the place was packed with the drunken spill-over from the nearby bars. There were mostly preppy college kids, assholes who couldn't handle their liquor, carrying on, trying to pick up the tired, haggard wait-resses. Frank and I sat at a table for two on the side, next to the windows. Frank ordered a cup of coffee and a piece of apple pie. I was famished, and since the meal was on Frank anyway, I decided to pig out. I ordered pancakes, scrambled eggs, hash browns, sausage, bacon, and a side order of French toast.

Frank went on and on, talking about Debbie. At first, I was zoning out, still pissed off about missing out on the chance of getting that money. Then I caught on as Frank was saying:

"...I mean how much longer can it go on like this? I think I've been very patient, as patient as anybody could be under the circumstances. I've tried to make her see a shrink, but she won't go. It's like all she cares about is making my life miserable."

"Dump her," I said.

"I'm going to," he said, "but it's not so easy. We've been together a long time—seven years."

"You wanna be married to her for seven more years?"

"No—of course not."

"Then tell her you want a divorce. Don't even think about it anymore. Just do it."

"You're right," he said. "That's what I'm gonna do—soon."

The waitress came with our food. I dug in, blocking out Frank again. I was so hungry I think I might've sucked in some bacon strips through my nose. But I started listening again when Frank said:

"So here's my offer to you, Tommy. After I divorce Debbie I'm gonna want a change of scenery. I don't think I'm ready to go into the sunset, but getting some sun might not be a bad idea. I'm sick of these cold

fucking winters—I figure I might give Arizona a shot.
I know I can't trust Gary to run the bar and I think
you've got a bigger head for business than him anyway.
But there's a condition involved—I'm not gonna turn
over the bar to you just like that. You have to prove
that you've quit gambling, and I mean *really* quit. No
more going to the racetrack or taking trips to Atlantic
City. I'm not gonna give you my bar for you to blow all
the money at the track. You go cold turkey or there's
no deal."

"But what about my acting career?" I asked.

"This is just something to fall back on," he said. "If
you get your big break and make it in Hollywood you
can say *sayonara* and I'll get somebody else to take
over. Believe me, I'll have no problem doing that. I
just think you're a good guy and you deserve a chance
to be successful and I want to help you any way I can.
So what do you say? Will you do it?"

"You mean it?" I said. "You're really gonna retire?"

"I never said the word 'retire.' Let's just call it a per-
manent vacation. I'll probably come back and forth to
New York and, who knows, maybe I'll open an Irish
bar in Arizona."

"Man, I can't believe this," I said. "You're really
asking me to run O'Reilley's?"

"I'm only doing this because I have faith in you,"
Frank said, "and because I know you're the one guy in
the world I can trust. And because I think you're the
best man for the job."

"Thanks a lot," I said. "Believe me—I won't let you
down."

While I finished eating, Frank told me more about his plans to divorce Debbie and to move to Arizona. I told Frank he would be happy out there and other things I knew would make him feel good. After Frank paid the bill at the register we went outside into the cold. Frank said he was going to take a cab home. We hugged goodbye, then I held open the door of the cab for Frank to get in.

I'd always liked walking the streets at night, especially in the winter. There was nobody around, not even any homeless people. Tonight I was thinking how crazy my life was. A few days ago I had nothing—now I was going to be the manager of a bar. Soon the days of getting turned down at audition after audition, feeling like a loser, were going to be gone for good. The new job would *help* me with the robbery too. Nobody would believe that the future manager of a bar would rob his own bar's Super Bowl pool.

Eight

The next day, Saturday, all I could think about was getting another crack at that safe. I was getting stir crazy sitting home so I decided to go to the gym to pump some iron.

Nowadays, I only worked out once or twice a week and sometimes I didn't go for a couple of weeks at a clip. It didn't really matter as far as work was concerned though because I had big muscles naturally and I always looked like I was in shape.

My gym was part of the Lenox Hill Neighborhood Association. It was a shitty gym, but it was cheap, running me only about three hundred bucks a year. I spent about an hour in the weight room, working my back and chest, then I went into the gym to play some pickup basketball. My team was losing and I was getting frustrated. This big blond guy tried to box me out for a rebound, pushing me back with his ass, so I took a swing at him, busting his lip. A few other guys broke up the fight, then the blond guy went to get some first aid. I played a few more games, then I jogged back to my apartment and took a shower.

I relaxed on my couch awhile, eating peanut butter sandwiches and watching college basketball, then at around five I got ready to go to work. Tonight, when I opened the safe, I was going to be prepared. I had a big black Hefty bag to put the money into so if anybody saw me leaving the bar they'd think I was just taking out some garbage.

At six o'clock I arrived at O'Reilley's. Gary was sitting at a table near the front of the bar. Right away I knew something was wrong. He looked up at me, then looked right back down at his plate of chicken wings.

"How's it goin'?" I said, but he still wouldn't look at me.

"Leave me the fuck alone," he said.

"Hey, don't get pissed off at me," I said. "Talk to your father if you got a problem."

"You're not running this bar," Gary said. "There's no fucking way. You don't know shit about running a bar. You're just some idiot bouncer."

I grabbed Gary by his shirt and lifted him out of his seat.

"Let me go," he said.

"Watch it," I said. "Just watch it."

I let Gary go and went to the back to hang up my coat. I was mad for a while, then I got over it. Gary was a jealous fuck, but what difference did that make? Soon I'd be the manager of a bar and the owner of a race horse. What would he be?

I already had it planned out—on Monday I'd call Alan Schwartz and set up a time I could meet with him, Pete and the other guys. Then I'd meet Bill Tucker and the other big shots at the racetrack and my life would be completely different.

I was in a good mood again when Kathy came over

to talk to me at the door. I could tell something was wrong. She was hanging her head and her shoulders were drooping.

"Cheer up," I said. "It's the weekend."

"I didn't get the part."

"Part? What part?"

"You know—in that play I told you about…at the Manhattan Theatre Club."

I stared at her for a couple of seconds and then it clicked.

"Oh, right. Sorry about that, Kath. That's too bad."

"My agent says they probably had this other woman in mind all along. She was in two plays at the MTC last year and the director likes her."

"I guess there's nothing you can do about it," I said.

"I know," she said, "it's just so frustrating. I knew I could be great in that role, but I guess it just wasn't meant to be. Anyway, I was at this bookstore on the West Side before, looking at plays, and there's this old Lanford Wilson play—you know, a one-act—and I think it would be great for our showcase."

"I wanted to talk to you about that," I said. "I'm not gonna be doing that showcase with you."

"What do you mean? Why not?"

"Because I'm just not. I'm sorry."

"I don't understand. What's going on?"

"Nothing's going on. I just don't want to do the showcase."

"But why? I mean if we get producers to come down maybe we could—"

"Come on, I don't want to argue with you about it,

all right? I'm not doing the showcase. If you want to do it, you can, but I'm not doing it."

She looked at me, shaking her head, then she walked away to take somebody's order. I felt sorry for her. She'd probably be a waitress until some guy came along and asked her to marry him. Then she'd quit acting and realize she'd never had the talent to make it in the first place. She'd be in her mid-thirties, her looks fading, feeling like she'd wasted her youth. I wished there was a way I could help her see the light sooner.

It was a packed Saturday night crowd and people were lined up outside the bar all night long in the wind and cold. Usually, a busy night would be a big pain in the ass, but tonight I was in a good mood, joking around with everybody.

At around two o'clock, when the crowd started thinning out, I started thinking about the safe. It was like when I make a big bet at the track and I'm staring at the starting gate, totally focused, like me and the starting gate are the only two things in the world. You could have taken away the bar and all the people and put me in the middle of an empty street with that safe and I wouldn't have known the difference. Frank came to me at the door and asked me if I was feeling all right, that I looked "out of it tonight." I told him I was fine, but I thought I might be coming down with a cold. Frank walked away and I realized I had to act more like my usual self. I didn't want Frank getting any ideas about me tomorrow when that money was missing.

Then I had a big break—Frank told me he was planning to go home early tonight.

"I don't think I've shaken my cold yet either," he said. "I think I'm gonna get home and get some rest. You leave early too—the flu's going around and it's a nasty one this year. Gary and the guys from the kitchen'll do the cleaning up tonight."

It was like Frank was on my side, helping me rob him. Kathy left early too, so all I had to do was get Gary out of the bar and I'd be set. But, it turned out, I didn't have to worry about Gary either. I watched Frank go to the bar and talk to Gary. The music was loud so I couldn't hear what they were saying, but it wasn't hard to guess. Frank was telling Gary to stay late and clean tonight and Gary was obviously pissed off. He said something and walked away. A few minutes after Frank left, Gary went home. There was nobody around to work the bar so I took over. It was closing time soon anyway and the crowd was clearing out.

I couldn't believe how everything was working out for me. It was almost too easy, like it was some kind of trap. Maybe I moved the money around last night and Frank noticed. Maybe he set up some hidden camera behind the bar and he was going to catch me red-handed.

Stop being so paranoid. Just steal the fucking money.

I flashed the lights for last call. There were mostly single guys left in the bar, all trying to hit on these two drunk girls. To speed things along, I told the two girls that I wasn't going to serve them any more beer. This got the girls out of the bar in a hurry—they were prob-ably going to one of the bars down the block that stayed open later—and most of the guys soon followed.

Finally, about ten minutes later, the last guy left the bar and I locked the door. The music was still playing—Hootie & The Blowfish—but I was alone in the room. I went right behind the bar to the safe and got down on my knees. I missed a digit in the combination and whispered "Fuck," biting down so hard on my bottom lip I tasted blood. My hands were shaking. Finally, the safe door opened and the money was still there, looking exactly like it did yesterday. Moving fast, like a bank robber, I put the bills in the Hefty bag. It took about thirty seconds, then I stood up, holding the bag of money. Nobody was there and Hootie was still singing. I was about to just leave, get the hell out of there, when I realized I didn't have my coat. Fuck. Taking the Hefty bag with me, I went down the corridor to where my black leather coat was hanging in a closet near the bathroom. I put on my coat and walked back toward the front of the bar. When I got to the door, I turned around, sensing someone behind me. Rodrigo was there, scrubbing the bar with a rag. I could've just left, but I didn't think this was a good idea. If I took off in a hurry, without saying anything, it might not look good tomorrow.

Trying to smile, I said, "Don't you work hard enough in the kitchen?"

Rodrigo looked up like he was seeing me in the room for the first time.

"Frank tells me to clean the bar tonight," Rodrigo said with his Mexican accent.

"Yeah, well Frank should pay you double your salary for doing that," I said. I could tell Rodrigo couldn't understand what I was saying so I rubbed my fingers together and said, *"Mas dinero."*

"Yes, *mas dinero*," Rodrigo said smiling.

"Well, I'm gonna drop this garbage out on the street and go home. Take it easy. *Adios.*"

"Adios," Rodrigo said.

At home, I dumped the stacks of bills onto the kitchen table and started counting the money. I counted the bills at least three times and got the same total— fourteen thousand dollars even.

Nine

I was too pumped up to fall asleep so I sat on my bed in the dark watching *Perry Mason* and some old John Wayne movie. Finally, I conked out.

When I woke up, around noon, I went right to the bag of money and counted the bills. I counted them again, then I put the bag away in the closet.

It was another nasty day— a mix of rain, sleet and snow—and I didn't feel like going anywhere. My muscles were still sore from working out and playing basketball and I figured I'd just hang out at home and watch the football games on TV. I ordered two sausage heros with extra onions from a pizza place on First Avenue, then I called the Korean deli and ordered two six-packs of Sam Adams, two containers of barbecue-flavored Pringles, and three of the little carrot cakes I liked.

There's nothing better than sitting on your couch on a nasty day, stuffing your face with great food and watching football. During halftime of the twelve-thirty game I got hungry again so I ordered some chicken wings—abusive-style—and a side order of cheese fries.

At five o'clock, I showered, then I got dressed and left for work. The rain and snow had stopped. It was dark, but it wasn't as cold as it had been the past few nights. I walked down First Avenue with my leather coat wide

open. I was thinking about tomorrow morning. I'd call
Alan Schwartz at about nine o'clock—set up a time to
meet the guys. Or maybe I'd throw Pete a call from
the bar tonight, just to make sure everything was still
cool.

A block away I spotted two police cars double-
parked in front of O'Reilley's. I wasn't surprised. I knew
that Frank would call the cops as soon as he noticed
the money was missing. I just hoped that Rodrigo
wouldn't rat on me. I didn't see why he would—he was
a good guy, an *amigo*—but I was still worried about it.

Looking in the window, I saw that the bar was
crowded—a lot more crowded than it usually was on
a Sunday at six o'clock. O'Reilley's didn't have big-
screen TVs so we usually didn't get a big football crowd
on Sundays like the sports bars did. I took a deep breath
and went inside.

I was expecting the cops to come over to talk to me
right away, but this didn't happen. Instead, people
hardly noticed me. Frank was in the middle of the
crowd and people were shouting at him and the police
—two male cops, one female cop, and one older guy in
a jacket and tie—were trying to calm everybody down.

Frank saw me behind the crowd and I made a face
to him that said, "What the hell's going on?" Frank
pushed his way through the crowd and came up to me.

"What happened?" I asked.

"Somebody robbed the safe."

"The safe? You're fuckin' kiddin' me. How the fuck
did—holy shit, you mean the Super Bowl money—?"

"Fourteen grand," Frank said. "I'm such an idiot for leaving money like that lying around. I was gonna go to the bank on Friday, but I figured it could wait till Monday."

"Jesus, I can't fuckin' believe this," I said, shaking my head. "When the hell did this happen?"

"We don't know. Last night…this morning. I just found out an hour ago."

"So what'd they do, bust the safe open?"

"Nah, they went in and out—used the combination. And I have a good idea who did it."

"Who?" I asked.

"Gary," Frank said. "Who else? He's the only one who knows the combination besides me and he was pretty upset last night when I told him I was gonna let you manage the bar. I wasn't gonna call the cops on him, but I figured I had to, with all this money gone. The thing is I just can't believe he'd do something like this—steal from his own father."

One of the male police officers came over and said something to Frank and then Frank introduced me to the officer. I was trying to look as pissed off as Frank.

The officer said he wanted to have the detective ask me a few questions and I said that was fine with me. While he went to get the detective I was looking over at the female cop. She was about thirty with short blond hair and blue eyes. She was very good looking.

"Tommy Russo."

Still looking at the blond cop, it took me an extra second or two to realize that the detective was talking to me. He was standing next to me—a guy about my height, but he was built like a rail and he was about fifty years old. He had a shiny bald head.

"Detective Edwards," he said as we shook hands. "I take it you're Tommy Russo."

"That's right," I said.

"And you're the bouncer here, is that correct?"

I nodded.

"Can you tell me what time you left the bar last night?"

"Around three o'clock," I said. "I know because I was home in bed by three-fifteen."

"Was Gary O'Reilley still here when you left?"

"Nah, he left about a half hour before me."

"So was there anybody here when you left the bar last night?"

"Just the guys from the kitchen, I guess," I said. "I thought I was coming down with something and I wanted to get to bed."

"Did you lock up the bar?"

"Nah, like I said, there were still guys around in the kitchen. I figured they'd lock up."

Frank had come over toward me and the detective during my last answer and now he was listening to us.

"When you were leaving," the detective said to me, "did you see anybody suspicious outside the bar?"

I shook my head. Then, just as the detective was about to ask me another question, I said, "Come to think of it, I *did* see Gary hanging out near the bar."

Now Frank and the detective were listening with wide-open eyes.

"And what time was this?" the detective asked.

"Right when I was leaving," I said. "I didn't think anything of it at the time—figured he was waiting to meet somebody—but now, come to think of it, it was kind of weird. I mean what the hell was he doing standing out there in the cold? He was like about ten yards up the block and he was just standing there with his hands in his pockets, looking down. I guess I figured he was waiting to meet one of his friends. Anyway, I said, 'What's up?' or something like that, but he didn't say anything to me so I just kept walking and went home."

When I finished talking, the detective stared at me for an extra second or two, but I didn't flinch.

"Thanks a lot," he said. "You're gonna be around here for a while, right?"

"I'm just starting my shift," I said smiling.

"Good," he said. "I might have to talk to you again in a little bit."

The detective walked away. I was proud of myself. I could've started making up stories—said Gary was still in the bar last night when I left, or that I saw him going into the safe. But what if Rodrigo or somebody else from the kitchen saw Gary leave? It would've made me look like I was lying, like I was trying to hide something. This way I looked even more innocent because why would I admit leaving the bar after Gary if I robbed the safe?

Then I noticed Frank, standing there, shaking his head.

"Don't worry about it," I said, putting a hand on his

back. "There's nothing you can do about it now anyway."

"How could a son do something like this to his father?" he said. "Huh? How could he?"

I'd never seen Frank looking so beat up. Even when Debbie was cursing him out to his face, humiliating him, he never looked like he was about to start crying.

I really felt bad for putting him through all this.

"Where's Gary now?" I asked.

"Home, I thought," Frank said. "The cops are out now, trying to find him."

"They better find our fuckin' money too," a guy who was listening in shouted. He was a big muscle-head Irish guy with red hair and a mustache. I'd seen him before. He was a regular of O'Reilley's day crowd.

"Don't worry about it," Frank told the guy and other people who were standing around. "Like I told you all before—if the money isn't recovered, I'll reimburse the pool out of my own pocket. The pool is one-hundred percent guaranteed."

"So who do you think did it?" the guy asked. "Your fuckin' kid?"

"It doesn't matter who took the money," Frank said, "all right? I said I'll back the pool, so what difference does it make to anybody? Just forget about it—it's over with."

The group of guys walked away, shouting about the robbery. When they were out of earshot Frank whispered to me, "I better talk to Gary—tell him no matter what happened last night to forget coming down here for a few days. One of these goons'll kick the living crap out of him if he took that money or not."

Frank went to his office to try to call Gary and I went behind the bar and poured myself a pint of Sam Adams. I saw Kathy talking to the detective. She looked in my direction for a second, then turned away quickly. She was probably still upset at me for backing out of that showcase.

The blond cop was standing near the door, talking to the other cops. We made eye contact and I thought I saw her smile. She wasn't wearing makeup, but she didn't need to. She had smooth pale skin and blond hair cut short around her ears.

She looked over at me again. This time we both smiled. She headed in my direction.

"Excuse me." She had a heavy Bronx accent, which kind of surprised me. I looked at her name tag—Officer Cheryl Lewis. "Sorry to bother you, but can you do me a favor?"

"Sure thing," I said smiling.

"Please don't touch anything back there, especially not the safe," Cheryl said. "We're gonna be dusting for prints in a minute."

I watched her walk back to the detective.

One of the male cops came over and started dusting the safe and all around it with a little brush and white powder. I took my beer around to the other end of the bar, trying to act like I didn't care what was going on. Meanwhile, my heart was racing out of control. Finally, the cop who was dusting told the detective he couldn't find a good print. Then, looking past the detective, I saw Rodrigo standing there. I didn't know if he just came in or if he'd been there the whole time. Rodrigo was short and there were a lot of big people in the bar so I could've missed him. The way he was staring at me I couldn't tell what he was thinking. Finally, he walked away into the kitchen.

I finished my beer and poured another. With Frank still back in his office trying to get in touch with Gary, there was nobody to man the bar so I took over and filled a couple of orders.

The detective came over to me at the bar and gave me his business card. He told me that if, by any chance, Gary showed up before the police found him, that it would be "in his interest" to give the detective a call. Then the detective and the cops left the bar.

I finished my beer and took a few more orders, making a few more bucks in tips. Frank came out from the back and said that he just got a call from Gary. The police found him in the Village and they were going to bring him in for questioning. Frank told me he was going to meet Gary at the precinct and he asked me if I'd work the bar while he was gone. I said this was no problem. Then, after Frank left, I asked Pedro, a Dominican busboy, to watch the bar for a few minutes because I had to go to the john. Instead, I went to the kitchen and saw Rodrigo there, making hamburgers. I made sure the door was closed and that no one was hanging around outside. Then I went over to Rodrigo and said, "Thanks a lot for that, buddy. I really owe you one."

"No problem," Rodrigo said. "You're my friend. I always give help for my friend."

"Just like the Beatles," I said.

Rodrigo looked confused.

"It was a joke—forget about it," I said.

I hugged Rodrigo, slapping him on the back.

"For this," I said, "I'm gonna give you a lifetime of free English lessons. Anything you want, just ask me."

I let Rodrigo go and started to walk away.

Then he said, "Tommy."

I stopped and turned around. Suddenly, I had a bad feeling in my stomach.

"Yeah," I said.

"You know I am very poor," he said. "I have very big family and we are very poor."

"I know that," I said. "You told me all about how bad your life was in Mexico."

"Yes, life in Mexico is very bad," he said. "So if we have more money, that is very nice. Because we are very poor family."

"What are you trying to say?"

"I no say anything. I just saying to you my family is very poor. We have nothing—no money. Maybe you give me some money because I don't talk to the *policia*. Because we are friends."

"Are you trying to blackmail me, Rodrigo?"

He looked at me, confused again. Maybe he didn't know what "blackmail" meant, but he knew how to do it.

"You know in America blackmail is against the law," I said. "It's not a very nice thing to do to your friends either."

"No blackmail," Rodrigo said. "I just want some more money—for my family."

I waited a few seconds, then I said, "All right. I'll give you five hundred bucks tomorrow night. But that's all you get, *entiende*?"

"One thousand dollars," he said in suddenly clear English.

"A *thousand*?" I said. I looked over my shoulder to make sure nobody was coming, then I said, "You got some pair of balls on you, you know that?"

Rodrigo looked confused again.

"Balls," I said, grabbing my crotch. *"Cojones."*

"You have some *cojones* too," he said.

We stared at each other for a few more seconds.

"All right," I finally said, "but you better keep your fuckin' mouth shut. I'm serious. I don't want you telling your wife about this or anybody else. *Comprende*?"

He nodded.

I walked out of the kitchen.

Ten

I guess you could say it was a quiet Sunday night at O'Reilley's. After the small football crowd left there were only a few customers left in the bar. I hung around most of the night sitting on a stool, drinking beer and watching TV.

Around nine o'clock, Frank showed up. He looked pissed off and went right back to his office without saying anything to anybody. I wanted to find out how things went at the precinct, but I decided it probably wasn't a good idea to bother him now. So I just stayed at the front of the bar, watching TV, figuring Frank would come talk to me when he was ready.

Finally, Frank came out front. He poured himself a pint of Guinness, then sat on a stool in front of me.

"So what happened?" I asked.

"They let Gary go," he said.

"Really? That's great, huh?"

"They still think he did it, but of course I didn't want to press charges and they couldn't prove anything anyway. He still swears he had nothing to do with it."

Frank took a long sip of his drink then put the glass back down on the bar.

"So that's great news," I said. "Isn't it?"

"You tell me."

"Maybe he didn't do it," I said. "Maybe they'll catch the guy who did now."

"I doubt that very much."

"Why's that?"

"Because I think they already had the guy who did it—Gary. It figures he'd do something like this to get back at me. And, believe me, he was the only person who knew the combination to the safe." Frank took another sip, then said, "This whole thing's my fault. I wanted to install security cameras in here for years, but I never got around to it. Now I got burned."

"So what happens now?" I asked.

"I forget about it, what else? Maybe in a few days Gary'll confess and give back the money. That kid has always been the biggest pain in my ass—I wish he'd just grow up already. You should've seen him at the precinct—making up stories, telling the cops he had nothing to do with this. It was the same way when he was in school—he'd get in trouble and I'd have to leave work and go meet him in the principal's office. He'd sit there lying, making a goddamn fool out of me."

"Let me take a wild guess," I said. "He told the cops I did it."

Frank nodded.

"I knew it," I said. "Sorry, Frank. I know he's your kid and all, but this really pisses me off."

Frank was looking at me funny.

"I hate to say this to you, Tommy, but I just have to get it over with and that'll be the end of it. I know you'd never do something like this in a million years. Even with your gambling the way it is I know how much respect you have for me. What I mean is I know you'd never—"

"Hold up," I said. "You think I—"

"Of course I don't."

"Good. I'm glad."

"But I just have to ask you anyway—to get it out of my system. I know you'd never steal from me, that you're not the type of guy who'd do something like that."

"Then why are you asking me?"

"Because I have to hear it—from your own mouth."

"Come on –"

"Just tell me you didn't take that money and I'll never say a word about it again."

I let out a deep breath, then I said, "I didn't take that money, and if you don't believe me you've got more problems than I thought."

"Thank you," Frank said. "That's all I needed to hear."

I got home at around two in the morning and went right to sleep. When I woke up I felt like I had closed my eyes two seconds ago, but sun was shining into my apartment. I looked at my clock and saw it was past nine o'clock. I got out of bed and called Alan Schwartz.

His snobby secretary answered. I had to go through a whole routine, explaining who I was five times, just to get her to transfer me. Then Alan came on the line.

"Hey, Alan—Tommy Russo."

The line was quiet for a few seconds, then he said, "Oh right, Tommy, how are you?" like I was his biggest buddy in the world.

"Not bad," I said. My voice sounded cranky from sleeping. "I just thought we could set up a time to get together, you know—meet."

"Did you get those forms my secretary sent you?"

"Nah, they didn't come yet," I said. "But I have the money."

"Terrific," Alan said. "I have an idea. It so happens I'm meeting Pete, Rob and Steve—I don't know if Pete told you about Rob and Steve—they're the other guys in the syndicate. Anyway, the four of us are getting together for lunch this afternoon at a restaurant near my office. I don't know what your schedule's like today, but if you want to make it a fivesome—"

"Of course I can make it," I said.

Alan gave me the name of a Chinese restaurant on John Street.

"That's right up the block from the OTB, right?"

"Pete was right," Alan said, "you *are* a real racing fan."

He told me they were meeting at one o'clock. I said "no problem" and hung up.

I put on some sweats and took a walk to the diner around the corner. I had the bacon, eggs and hash browns special, then I came home and shit my brains out. I'd had it with cheap diner food. From now on I was going to go out to good restaurants or cook at home.

I took a long shower then I came out and searched through my closet. I wanted to look good today, but I couldn't find anything to wear. I hadn't gone clothes shopping in a long time and I realized that I'd have to hit Barney's or Macy's one of these days, spend a few bucks on some nice outfits, maybe pick up a few pinstriped suits and some button-down shirts with cufflinks.

But for today what I had in my closet would have to do. I put on a pair of beige slacks, a white shirt, a black sports jacket, and a pair of brown dress shoes. The shoes needed shining, I'd taken the shirt out of my dirty laundry pile, and the slacks and jacket were wrinkled. Unfortunately, I didn't own an iron so I put the pants and jacket on as they were and I scrubbed down my shoes with an old pair of underwear. I was going to shave, but then I figured I'd look classier with a little five o'clock shadow. I put on a gold chain and unbuttoned the top three buttons of my shirt. When I was all set to go, I stared at myself in the bathroom mirror.

I wasn't in the horse business yet, but I definitely looked the part.

I took the 6 train to the Brooklyn Bridge. It was sunny and not nearly as cold as it had been the past few days. I walked around the traffic circle near City Hall Park, my leather coat open wide, a gym bag with ten thousand dollars over my shoulder. It was only 12:20 and I had forty minutes to kill so I just walked around the Wall Street area, window-shopping. Finally, at around one o'clock, I cut back up to the restaurant on John Street.

Pete was sitting at a table with two other guys. When he saw me coming he stood up and shook my hand.

"Long time no see," I said. But I really wanted to say, Long time no smell.

He looked just about the same as the last time I saw him. He still had that big mole on his chin, but it looked like he'd plucked the hairs out of it. And he still had that awful B.O.

Pete said Alan was running a little late at his office and he introduced me to Rob and Steve. They were both short and weaselly looking. Rob had gray hair, but his face didn't look old, and Steve had dark hair, but he looked older than Rob. They were both wearing shirts and ties.

I put my coat over the back of my chair and the gym bag down on the floor. There were two empty seats— I sat in the one farthest away from Pete. We started bullshitting. Rob worked at a bank, doing something with computers, and Steve was an accountant. They asked me what I did and I told them, "I used to be an actor—now I'm a horse owner."

Everybody laughed, then Pete said, "Tommy works at a bar on the Upper East Side."

"Cool," Steve said. "What do you do there?"

Before I could say, I manage the bar, Pete said, "He's a bouncer."

I shot Pete a look, upset that he'd brought that up.

"The Upper East Side," Rob said to me, "my old stomping grounds. What bar do you bounce at?"

I was about to tell him when Pete said, "Here's the man of the hour."

Alan Schwartz was coming toward our table. He looked like he sounded on the phone. What I mean is he looked rich. He was wearing a black overcoat over a gray suit. I didn't know much about clothes unless I was looking at the labels, but his suit looked like it had cost him a nice chunk of change. He had a rich face too. His skin was tan and his brown hair was slicked back. But for some reason I remember his eyebrows most. They were so thin and neat they looked like they were drawn with pencil.

I stood up and shook Alan's hand.

"A pleasure," he said. He had a firm handshake and he looked at my eyes until he let go.

The waitress came around and we all ordered. My stomach was still hurting from breakfast so I took it easy, ordering the pepper steak and a side of pork dumplings.

When the waitress left we started talking horses. Rob, it turned out, was a big poker player and he told me a story about a game he was in down in Atlantic City at Caesar's Palace. Then Steve told me how he was down in Florida last week, visiting his mother at a condo, and he made it over to Gulfstream Park a couple of times and hit a triple for two thousand dollars. I told him about the last time I was in Florida, six years ago, and how I hit Calder, Pompano Park, Tampa Bay Downs and a few dog tracks. Our food came and we kept bullshitting about gambling and horse racing. We started talking about next year's Triple Crown races and the new crop of three-year-olds.

Sitting there, talking horses, I felt like I belonged. When I was at the bar, checking IDs, or at auditions with all those phony pretentious wannabes, I felt out of place. But sitting here, with a bunch of guys who loved horse racing, I felt like I fit right in. I even thought

Alan was cool, definitely not as stuck-up and into himself as I'd thought he was.

"We should probably get down to business," Alan said, then he waited until everybody at the table stopped talking and was paying attention to him. "As everyone here probably already knows, Tommy here is the fifth and final person on our little ownership team. Just to update you, Tommy, we're planning to claim our first horse next week. Bill Tucker, the trainer we're planning to use, has been watching a few horses in the twenty-five to thirty-five range and when he's ready to put a slip into the claiming box he'll let us all know. Now what else did I want to discuss? Ah, yes, insurance. I spoke with several—"

"Can I just ask you one question?" I said.

"Of course you can, Tommy. What is it?"

"You were talking about Bill Tucker. When do we meet him?"

"Well, we all met Bill a few weeks ago out at Aqueduct," Alan said. "But we'll all meet him again when we go to the track to claim the horse."

"And about the horse," I said. "You said Tucker has a few horses he's watching. Do we get to help decide which one he claims?"

"We've discussed that already," Alan said, "and if you don't have a strong objection we'd prefer to leave that decision up to Bill Tucker. The way we figured it, we're not down at the track every day, watching the horses train, so we might as well leave the hands-on decisions to someone who knows more about the business than we ever will. It's like owning a baseball team. When the owner starts jumping in, making decisions for the manager, the whole team gets screwed up. But when the manager makes the on-the-field decisions the team has a chance of winning."

I asked Alan which horses Tucker was thinking about claiming and he told me the names. I'd heard of all of them, except the one Tucker liked the most—a filly named Sunshine Brandy. She had a great pedigree, Alan explained—her grandfather was out of Secretariat—and she'd recovered from physical problems that had plagued her early in her career. She had done most of her racing down in Louisiana, which explained why I never heard of her. Tucker thought that if we could claim her for thirty or thirty-five grand it would be a steal.

Alan started to talk about insurance again, then I said, "I have one more question. Let's say we claim the horse for thirty-five K. We have fifty K in the pool total, right? So what happens to the other fifteen Gs?"

"Good question," Alan said. "Training costs, insurance, a lot of other expenses that the packet I'm going to give you will get into more. You know owning a race horse isn't inexpensive. Owning just one horse could cost as much as twenty grand a year with various fees and expenses. Hopefully the horse'll be making some money so we can get some of that back, but we also have a bimonthly billing plan worked out that we'll adjust against any profits at the end of the year."

Everybody was talking at once and I was busy daydreaming about what it would feel like to be a horse owner, to sit in one of those owner's boxes, smoking a cigar.

Then I heard Alan say, "Before we go I just have to say something that needs to be said and if no one else is going to say anything then I will." He was quiet for a couple of seconds, then he looked at Pete and said, "I really don't want to embarrass you, but I've brought this up with you before and you haven't done anything about it so I have to say something again. Can you do us all a favor and start wearing some deodorant?"

Rob and Steve were trying not to laugh and I thought it was pretty funny too.

"What?" Pete said, sniffing his underarm. "I don't smell."

"I don't want to argue about it," Alan said. "You might not think you smell, but other people think you smell, and if other people think you smell then you smell."

Rob and Steve couldn't hold back anymore and they started laughing hysterically. Alan was smiling too, but I could tell he was really upset.

"Nobody else thinks I smell," Pete said to Alan. "You're the only one who thinks I smell."

"Do we really have to go through this at every meeting?" Alan said.

"I don't smell," Pete said. "If I smelled wouldn't my wife say something to me?"

"Maybe she smells too," Rob said. Now I couldn't hold back—I started cracking up, and Alan started laughing too. The only person who wasn't laughing was Pete.

"Hey, don't make jokes about my wife," Pete said.

"Come on," Rob said. "Where's your sense of humor?"

"Seriously," Alan said to Pete. "Why can't you put on some deodorant?"

"Because I don't smell," Pete said, "and I'm sick of you guys saying I do."

"All right, you want to get an objective opinion," Alan said. Then he looked at me and said, "Tommy, your honest opinion—do you think Pete smells?"

I played it good—with perfect comic timing. Everybody at the table got quiet. Then I looked at Pete, staring him down, and said, "Like a hot piece of shit."

Everybody at the table laughed, including Pete. I really liked these guys a lot.

Finally, we all settled down. Pete said he'd start wearing some cologne if it would make everybody happier. The waiter came to take our dessert orders. I was handling my food pretty good so I ordered two scoops of vanilla ice cream.

The waiter came back and put the desserts on the table. We were all laughing it up, having a good time, then I said to Alan, "Before I forget—I want to give you the money. You know, the ten grand."

"Oh, right," Alan said. "I guess that's a good idea."

I reached under the table, picked up the gym bag, and started to pass it across the table to Alan. Everybody stopped eating and was looking at me.

"What's this?" Alan asked.

"It's a gym bag," I said, "but don't worry—it's been laying around my closet forever. Toss it out when you get home—I don't need it."

"I don't mean the gym bag," Alan said. "I mean what's *inside* it?"

"The ten grand," I said, wondering what the big problem was.

"You brought *cash*?" Alan said.

"Yeah," I said. "You told me to, didn't you?"

Alan smiled.

"This is a joke, right?" he said.

"No, what kind of joke would this be? You told me to bring you the money, I brought you the money."

"I thought you'd bring a check."

"I don't write checks," I said.

"Then a money order, whatever. I can't accept your money in cash."

"Why not?"

"Because I can't."

"It's real money," I said. I unzipped the bag and took out some wads of bills. "See?"

"What did you do," Rob said, "rob a bank?"

"What do you mean?" I said, wondering what everybody's big problem was.

"That's a lot of cash to be walking around town with," Pete said.

"I took it out of the bank this morning," I said. "Alan told me on the phone to bring the money."

"We just had a little misunderstanding," Alan said. "It's no big deal. We know you're serious now and that you're good for the money. I don't think anyone will object if you get me a check later in the week."

Now I knew what was going on—Alan was just trying to bust my chops, pulling a power trip. Maybe my first impression of him was right after all. If I'd brought my checkbook he probably would've said, "Sorry, I only take cash." Uppity bastard. Well, there was no way I was going to screw around with checks or money orders. I wasn't stupid. I knew if I went to the bank or post office with hot money, started filling out slips, it couldn't lead to anything good.

"Money is money," I said. "Why don't you just take it the way I brought it, and that'll be the end of it?"

"Because this is a business transaction," Alan said. He wasn't yelling, but his voice was getting louder. "I need a check for accounting purposes. I'm not going to go to the bank and deposit ten thousand dollars in cash."

"Look," I said, "let's not make a big deal about this, all right? Just take the money."

"I can't accept cash," Alan said.

"Why not?"

"Because I can't. Weren't you listening to me? Are you some kind of idiot?"

I was about to jump over the table and bust Alan's head open.

"Hey, cool down guys, Jesus," Pete said. "So there was a little misunderstanding—what's the big deal? I know what we'll do—I'll take the money. I'll deposit it in my account and write Alan a check directly. Then, Alan, you can write Tommy out a receipt for your records. How's that sound?"

"I guess that's all right with me," Alan said. "If you feel like doing that."

"How does that sound to you, Tommy?"

"I don't have a problem with that."

"Anybody else have an objection?"

Steve and Rob shook their heads.

"Good, then the issue's resolved," Alan said. "See, that wasn't too hard, was it? Christ, maybe the MSG from this food is going to all your heads."

Steve or Rob, I forget who, laughed. I was still looking at Alan, trying to figure out why he was being such a dick.

While we finished our desserts, Alan just talked like Mr. Know-It-All about "finances" and "insurance." I knew he was just trying to show everybody up, talking about what *he* knew. I could've done the same thing if I started talking about acting or working in a bar. I wanted to see him read a line from a script or try to explain how to make a Long Island Iced Tea. Finally, Alan said he'd be calling everybody in a couple of days to tell us what was going on with Bill Tucker. There was a chance Bill might want to claim a horse later this week or early next week and Alan said that if that happened we'd all meet down at the racetrack to watch the horse run. The check came and we split it evenly. Usually, I didn't have a problem splitting checks, but Alan's part of the bill was five bucks more than everybody else's and you'd think a big-shot Wall Street guy, probably with more money than he knew what to do with, could pay his own way.

Pete left the restaurant with me.

"Don't worry about Alan," he said when we were on the sidewalk. "He's a really great guy once you get to know him—hell of a stockbroker too. That's how I met him. He got me into Microsoft at thirty bucks a share." Pete laughed. "Anyway, you wait—you'll see what a great guy he is too. When I first met him we didn't really hit it off. He likes to do things his way and that's it. So—besides Alan—what do you think of the syndicate?"

"It all looks cool to me," I said. "I guess I owe you one."

"Ah, forget about it," Pete said. A strong wind blew down John Street. It seemed colder than before.

"Well, I better take off to the bank," Pete said. "This bag of money's getting heavy."

"Take it easy," I said.

Pete walked toward his car and I went the other way, toward the Broadway-Fulton Street subway station. For a while, I was still pissed off at Alan, but then I started to forget about him. I was officially part of a horse syndicate now, and I really didn't care about anything else.

Eleven

When I got off the subway at the Sixty-eighth Street station, instead of walking downtown toward my apartment, I headed in the opposite direction.

I knew Frank wasn't going to be home this afternoon. He'd told me last night that he was going to be busy all day today, meeting with distributors at the bar. I didn't feel like going home and sitting on the couch alone all afternoon, so I decided to celebrate my new career as a horse owner by visiting Debbie O'Reilley.

I'd never been to Frank's building before, but I passed it all the time. It was one of those classy, old doorman buildings on Seventy-second Street near Third Avenue. The doorman didn't seem very surprised to see a strange guy asking for Debbie O'Reilley in the middle of the afternoon. Maybe this was the time that most of her boyfriends came to visit. The doorman had to ring twice, then he said, "Tommy is here to see you," and he hung up the receiver and said to me, "Go right up—apartment 19B."

The inside of the building was even nicer than I thought it would be. The lobby had a big gold chandelier and there was red carpeting in the elevator. I got out on the nineteenth floor and walked along the wide hallway. I didn't even have to look for apartment 19B because Debbie was sticking her head out of the doorway, smiling at me.

The first thing I said to myself when I saw her was, What the hell am I doing here? Without makeup and with her hair wrapped up in a towel she looked like she could be my grandmother. But it wasn't her looks that bothered me as much as *her*. I remembered how I'd always hated her, how I thought she was just a nasty drunk who treated her husband, a great guy, like a piece of dog shit. The last thing I wanted to do was hurt Frank more than I already had, but there I was, about to fuck his wife.

She let me into the apartment. She was wearing a white terry cloth bathrobe and looked like she just came out of the shower.

"Well, *this* is a pleasant surprise," she said, looking at me the way she always looked at me at the bar, like I was a fresh piece of meat on the slab. From a few feet away I could smell the Scotch on her breath, so she'd already had at least one drink today. "And all dressed up too. Well, come inside. Make yourself at home."

We went into a big living room with black leather furniture. There were tall windows with a view downtown—in the distance, I could see part of the Empire State Building. Debbie sat down on the couch and I sat next to her.

"I'm very glad you're here," Debbie said. Her words were slurred slightly, but she wasn't smashed. "But, to be honest, I'm a little upset that you didn't let me know first. I would've gotten myself together for you —you know, put on some leather."

"That's all right," I said. "You look great just the way you are."

Debbie put her hand on my leg and smiled. She really was disgusting.

"All full of compliments," she said. "Well, thank you very much. But why are you being so nice to me all of a sudden?"

"What do you mean?"

"My memory gets a little fuzzy when I drink, but if I recall the last time we were together you were trying to break my arm."

"Sorry about that."

"That's all right—I'm sure I'll figure out a way for you to make up for it." She was rubbing my leg now. "So what made you change your mind?"

"What do you mean?"

"Oh, come on. Obviously you were never very interested in me before."

"I was just passing by so I decided to come up. But maybe you want me to go home."

"No, of course I don't want you to go. I just meant did you come here for a good time or because you find me irresistibly sexy?"

"I really don't know why I came here," I said.

"Well, at least you're honest," she said. "That's an unusual quality for a man." She moved her hand over my crotch, then said, "I could use something to drink. Can I get you something?"

"That's okay."

"Really? In that case I'll skip my drink too. I don't want to be on a different plane than you."

She was still rubbing my crotch.

I said, "So Frank's not around, right?"

"No, he's at the bar. We have the apartment all to ourselves for at least a few hours."

"Maybe it was a bad idea to come here—"

She grabbed my arm—holding it tightly. Then in a deeper, sexier voice she said, "What do you like?"

"Like?"

"I mean maybe you have a favorite fetish? Do you like to be spanked? Do you want mommy to tell you that you've been a very bad boy. What do you like?"

"I don't have any fetishes."

"Everybody has *some* fetish, a fantasy they've never experienced before. Something they've always wanted to do, but never tried. Maybe you like it rough."

She pinned me against the side of the couch and started kissing me. I felt her hard implants rubbing against my chest.

"This is what you want, isn't it? This is what you like."

I was looking into her dark brown eyes. She was kissing me, biting hard on my tongue. I tasted a mix of alcohol and blood. Her hands were under my shirt, her long fingernails scratching my chest.

"Come on, tell mommy you like it. Tell mommy you want it."

She continued to bite and claw me and I didn't stop her. Finally, she pulled me into the bedroom. I saw the wedding picture on the dresser. Frank was right— Debbie *did* look a lot better back then. I tried not to look at the picture again. I hated myself for being there behind Frank's back, and I hated Debbie for putting the idea into my head in the first place.

She pushed me down onto the bed and climbed on top of me with her drunk old lady's body—sucking hard on my neck with her teeth. I pushed her away—afraid she'd give me a hickey—but she pushed me back down hard and continued to have her way with me. She was strong for a woman—or maybe I just wasn't fighting back. She was holding down my arms, biting my nipples.

"You like it like this, don't you? Don't you?"

She unzipped my pants and tossed away her robe. I wondered how I ever could have thought she was sexy. Her thin, bony body disgusted me. I was looking up at her lumpy, sagging implants and her wrinkled face.

I closed my eyes, trying to shut everything out, but it didn't help. I saw myself tumbling down a steep flight of stairs. I felt like my head was going to explode.

I stood out of bed and started getting dressed.

"What's the matter?"

I didn't answer.

"I don't understand," she said. "What's wrong?"

"You better not tell anybody I was here," I said, facing the door. "I'm serious—you better not tell Frank."

"Tell Frank what? We didn't do anything. *Hardly* anything."

"Just keep your drunken mouth shut."

"Why?" she said, like she thought it was funny. "Don't you trust me?"

I slammed the bedroom door and left the apartment as fast as possible.

*

I woke up with a splitting headache. It was dark in my
apartment and I looked over at the digital clock and
saw it was a few minutes past five. It was strange because I felt like I'd only been asleep for a few minutes,
but a couple of hours had gone by. I really wasn't in
the mood to see Frank tonight. I wanted to call in sick
but, remembering about the robbery, I knew it wouldn't
look good if I suddenly stopped showing up for work.
Besides, I had to pay off Rodrigo. So I took a shower
and came out feeling okay, but not great. On the way
to work, I bought a large iced coffee at a deli and
gulped it down. Then I went to a pizza place and had a
couple of pepperoni slices and a calzone and I felt a lot
better.

I was glad it was Monday and that it would be slow
at O'Reilley's. I probably wouldn't even have to work
the door tonight. It was Gil's night off bartending so
I'd either help Gary out at the bar or just hang out,
drinking beer and watching TV.

When I walked into the bar Gary started yelling at
me. He had a big bandage on his forehead and under
one of his eyes he had a purple shiner. At first, I wasn't
paying attention to what he was saying. I was just
watching this crazy guy screaming at me. There were
only a few other people in the bar—holdovers from
the day crowd. They were looking at Gary pretty much
the same way I was.

"...so what are you gonna do, just stand there
looking stupid?" he said. "Let's go outside and settle
this like men. What's the matter, you're chickenshit?
You can steal money from a safe but you can't fight

me? Come on, I'm serious. I wanna kick your ass."

"Just go back to work," I said. "Stop making a dick out of yourself."

"You have two choices," Gary said. "Either you go outside and fight me like a man or you get the hell out of here."

"I don't wanna hurt you," I said.

"You don't want to hurt me, huh? Well, surprise, I'm already hurt. One of the guys whose money you stole from the football pool was somehow under the impression that I did it and he and a couple of his friends were waiting outside my apartment this morning. I'm not taking any more punches from anybody else. If you want to hurt me, you'll have to do it yourself."

"What the hell is going on here?" Frank had come from the back of the bar.

"Tommy and I are getting ready to fight this thing out, that's what's going on."

"Hey, come on, let's just cool it," Frank said. "Both of you."

"I didn't do anything," I said.

"Ha!" Gary said. "Why don't you go check his apartment? I bet you'll find fourteen thousand dollars there."

I smiled like I was innocent and Gary was crazy. I had my arms crossed in front of my chest.

"I'm not gonna have fighting in my bar," Frank said. "Now just get back to work and try to act like sensible human beings."

"Look at him," Gary said. "He has that money in his apartment, can't you tell? He thinks this is all a big joke."

"I don't have any money in my apartment," I said.

"Of course you don't—because you probably already gambled it away. I'm right, aren't I? You gambled that money away already, didn't you?"

"Get out of my face," I said.

Gary got past Frank and came up to me. He pushed me with both his hands but he didn't even budge me.

"Hey, that's enough now," Frank said, pulling Gary away. Frank pointed his index finger at Gary's face. "I'm serious now and this is the last time I'm telling you—I don't want any more of this bullshit in my bar."

"Tell *him* that," Gary said, looking at me. "He's the one who robbed you."

"Are you gonna get back to work or not?"

"Not with *him* here," Gary said.

"Then go home," Frank said. "Get the hell out of here."

Gary's face was red. He was sweating. He looked at me, then back at Frank, then at me again.

"Fuck you," he finally said to both of us.

He went to the back of the bar and came back wearing his winter coat. He pushed past me and left the bar.

Frank was shaking his head.

"Sorry about that everybody," he said. "Tommy, give everybody one on the house, okay?"

"You got it," I said.

When I finished serving everybody their free drinks I went over to Frank who was sitting on a stool at the end of the bar, sipping a pint of Guinness.

"I don't know how I'm supposed to feel," Frank said

to me. "As his father, I'm worried about him and I
don't want him to get hurt. On the other hand, if he
took that money I think he deserves to get knocked
around a little."

"*If* he took that money," I said. "So now you're not
sure?"

"I don't know what to believe," Frank said. "At least
Gary wasn't hurt too bad. He had to get some stitches
for his forehead, but the doctor said he probably won't
have a scar. Gary didn't want to report the whole thing
to the cops and I thought that was a pretty good idea
myself. I just want it to blow over."

Frank sat there for a few seconds, looking down at
his Guinness, then he said, "You mind handling the
bar alone tonight and closing up for me? It should be
pretty slow anyway—I'll probably be leaving early."

"No problem," I said.

"By the way, I had that little talk with Debbie before."

Hearing Debbie's name, coming out of Frank's
mouth, put a big knot in my stomach.

"A talk?" I said.

"Yeah. I told her I want a divorce and we're doing it
—we're splitting up."

"That's great," I said. "I mean that's what you want,
right?"

"No, what I want is Debbie to be the woman I married, but obviously that isn't possible."

"I'm proud of you, man," I said, leaning over the
bar and parting Frank on the back of his shoulder.
"Believe me, you don't need a woman like that in your

life. You're gonna be a lot better off without her."

"I didn't tell Gary about it yet so if he comes back here I'd appreciate it if you kept a lid on this."

"Hey, you know you can trust me," I said.

"Yeah, I know I can," Frank said. "Can I tell you something else?"

"Shoot," I said.

"I'm scared. I know how stupid that sounds, but it's the truth. I'm sixty-six years old and I'm scared shit to just pack up and start over again, but I'm gonna do it anyway. I'm gonna get on a plane in a few weeks and head out to Arizona and start looking for a place to live."

"That's the spirit," I said.

"I figured I might give Scottsdale a shot," he said. "They've got a lot of sports out there, with spring-training baseball and everything. Who knows? Maybe I'll open up an O'Reilley's West."

"If you do, can I come work for you?"

"I need you to manage this place."

"I know," I said. "I was just busting your chops."

Frank took another sip of Guinness, then said, "The only problem is I think I'm gonna get burned on my divorce settlement."

"Really?" I said. "Why's that?"

"Because I was stupid and I married Debbie without a prenup. I think that's why she didn't give me a hard time when I broke the news. I thought she'd start screaming and coming after me, but she just sat there calmly on the couch, like she was happy to hear I was leaving her. And if I was her I'd be happy about it too. The woman hasn't lifted a finger her whole life and now she's gonna wind up a rich old lady."

"How rich?" I asked.

"Oh, I don't know," Frank said. "The one thing I have going for me is the way she's been running around the past few years I don't think it'll be too hard for me to prove adultery. I already hired this detective to follow her around, see if he can get any dirt on her."

"A detective?"

"Yeah, he's supposed to start tomorrow. Nothing fancy—just two hundred bucks a day to see if he can get me a few pictures. What I'm gonna try to do, I think, is show her the pictures and then work out some out-of-court settlement. Maybe I'll offer her the apartment and some cash and see if she bites. But even if I have to split everything I own with her fifty-fifty it'll be worth it to get on with my life."

"That's cool," I said. "I mean I think you're doing the right thing."

"I'll drink to that," Frank said. He finished his Guinness, then said, "I really want to thank you, Tommy, I mean for listening to me, helping me see this thing straight. I know I'm not the most open guy in the world sometimes and I...I just want you to know you were a big help to me."

Frank's eyes were red and wet, like he might start to cry.

"Forget about it," I said.

I reached over the bar and patted him on the back, then I went to the bathroom to take a leak. As I was pissing I leaned over the urinal and banged my head against the wall. Going over to Debbie's today was temporary insanity. I was just lucky Frank's detective started tomorrow instead of today or he would've nailed me.

I looked at myself in the mirror. I had a big red spot on my forehead, but it didn't look like it would turn into a bump.

I washed up, then I went into the kitchen. Rodrigo was sitting on a stool reading one of his English books. I made sure no one else was around, then I took out the thick envelope with one thousand dollars in it.

"Here you go," I said. "Put it away and don't open it till you get home."

Rodrigo put the envelope inside the book and closed it.

"You can say thank you," I said.

"Thank you," he said.

"You're welcome."

I started to walk away.

"Tommy."

"What is it?" I said.

"Yesterday and today Frank and the police was talking to me," he said. "They have questions, a lot of questions. They ask me about the money, about the safe, about everything."

"So keep your mouth shut," I said. "That's what the envelope's for."

I was about to walk away when Rodrigo said, "I want another thousand."

I just stood there.

"Excuse me?"

"I want another thousand—tomorrow night."

"Look," I said. "There's a thousand bucks in that envelope and that's all you're gonna get."

"I want another thousand—tomorrow night," he said. "Or I say what I see to Frank and the police."

"Look, I didn't have to give you shit, all right?" I said. "It was very generous of me to give you that money. So why don't you just go home tonight and feel lucky?"

"I want another thousand—tomorrow night," Rodrigo said. "If you don't give the money for me, I go to tell Frank and the *policia*."

I walked over to him and looked him right in the eye. I smiled, shaking my head, then I gave him a quick right hook in the gut. When he keeled over I kneed him in the balls. I didn't want to hurt him, but if he wanted to play hardball with me what choice did I have? I pushed him back against the stove, forcing him to stand up straight. His face was red and he was trying to catch his breath.

Now my idea was to scare him, like I was a thug in the movies.

"Now listen to me, you little piece of shit," I said. "I'm not giving you another fuckin' cent and if you even think about telling anybody anything I'm gonna tell them *you* took the money. Who do you think they'll believe? I'm Frank's friend, I'm gonna be manager of this bar someday, but who are you? You're just a cook, an illegal alien. Don't think I forgot that. I'll make a few calls and you'll be back in Mexico, begging for food on the streets. Is that what you want? Huh? Is that what you want?"

I gave him another solid right in the gut, then I walked away, taking a handful of French fries out of the rack on my way out.

I almost choked on a bite of fries when I saw Janene sitting on a bar stool. She looked like she had come straight from work. She was wearing a dark blue jacket and a matching skirt and her legs were crossed. Her tote bag and her long black winter coat were on the stool next to her. Frank was in the same spot he was before, a few stools away from Janene, working on a new pint of Guinness. I knew I had to get Janene the hell out of the bar—fast. I didn't know why she was here, but I didn't want her going crazy again, talking about how I stole her jewelry with Frank sitting right there.

I went up to Janene and tapped her on the shoulder. Before she could say anything I said, "Let's do this outside."

"No, I want to—"

"Outside," I said.

"All right," she said. She got up, took her coat and bag, and started toward the door. I looked over at Frank, who was watching us, and rolled my eyes, like I was saying "Women." Frank smiled, knowing exactly what I meant.

When I went outside Janene had her coat on and she was standing with her hands on her hips. She had a full face of makeup and the yellow light of the bar's marquee was shining directly into her fake blue eyes.

"So what's up?" I asked.

"This is your last chance, Tommy. Give me back my jewelry or I'm going to the police."

"Hold up a second," I said. "Didn't we go through this already the other night?"

"I know you took it," she said, "so I don't want to hear any more stories."

"Look, I was nice to you the last time you came by here," I said, "but I'm not gonna put up with this shit anymore. I'm not gonna lose a job because you're coming around here all the time with these crazy ideas in your head."

"When I left here the other night, I wasn't sure," she said. "I thought, Okay, maybe I shouldn't've gone over there and accused him like that when I wasn't sure."

"You should've listened to yourself."

"But then I thought about it some more and I realized how ridiculous that was. You were the only one who could've done it, and the way you disappeared like that while I was sleeping—of course you did it. Why would you do something like this to me, Tommy? How could you?"

Janene looked like she was about to cry.

"Look," I said. "I told you I didn't wanna make a scene here—"

"Were you planning to do this all along?" she said. "Did you just want to get me in bed so you could rob me?"

"Of course not," I said. "I liked you a lot and, if you

wanna know the truth, I still like you. Like I said, I was just a little upset that you were married and didn't tell me about it, but I guess I can get over that. If you wanna keep going out with me, I have no problem with that— I mean I'd love to go out with you again sometime if that's what you want. I guess I shouldn't've left that night without waking you up. That's my fault—I apologize for that."

Janene stared at me for a few seconds, then she said, "You're serious. You really want to go out with me again?"

"Why not?" I said. "I thought we were pretty good together."

"What makes you think I'd want to go out with you?"

"It's up to you."

"Dating you was like a nightmare," she said. "Not only do I not want to go out with you—I never want to see you again."

"Then why do you keep coming back here?"

"To get my jewelry."

"I can't help you there," I said, "but if you want the hundred bucks I owe you I have that. Just stop by my place any time and I'll give it to you."

"I have a better idea," she said. "Maybe I'll go inside right now and tell your boss that you robbed me— see what he has to say about *that*."

I stood in front of her.

"Hold up," I said. "If you think I'm letting you go in there—"

"You can't stop me."

She was right—people were walking by, looking at us.

"Why do you need to tell my boss about this?"

"Maybe he'd like to know how his bouncer robbed me."

"So then maybe I get fired. How's that gonna help you?"

"You know, you're right," she said. "I have a better idea—I'll call the police."

She started to walk away. I knew I had to do something.

"Wait," I said.

She turned around and looked back at me. On cue, I started to cry. Well, I guess I wasn't really crying, but I did a good enough job of faking it. I turned around with my back facing her and then I put my hands over my face and made loud sobbing noises. It might've been the best acting performance of my life.

"What's the matter with you?" she asked.

My hands were wet with tears. Now I knew I had her.

"I'm sorry," I said. "I just can't help it."

"Help what?"

"Everything." I squeezed out a few more tears, then I said, "All right, you wanna know the truth? The truth is I took your fucking jewelry. You satisfied?"

"Where is it?"

"I don't have it."

"Why not?"

"I pawned it off for gambling money. I tried to buy

it back—I swear to fucking God I did—but the guy already sold it."

She stared at me for a few seconds then said, "For gambling money? What are you talking about?"

"I'm a compulsive gambler," I said, crying. "I didn't want to tell you about it, but it's the truth. I started betting in high school and it's gotten worse and worse since. I go to the racetrack and the OTBs all the time, betting on fucking horses. I'm sorry I didn't tell you about it—I just didn't know how to bring it up."

"But why?" she said. "Why did you steal from me?"

"Because I have a problem, that's why," I said. "I gamble too much—I get out of control. It's my fault, I know. I have no one to blame but myself."

"Why don't you go for help?"

"That's what I'm *gonna* do. I've thought about it before, but now I know, I *really* know I need it. I'm gonna go to Gamblers Anonymous—quit once and for all. Please, Janene. I don't know why I did it. I mean I liked you—I thought we had something special going. Then, as usual, I fucked everything up. But please, I'm begging you, please don't tell my boss any of this. I can't afford to lose my job. I'm begging you."

She was looking at me like I was her kid that she'd just spanked, and now she felt bad about it.

"How could you steal from me?" she said. "How could you do something like that to me, Tommy?"

"I was out of control—what can I say? But I have some good news—I won at the track with your money and I can pay you back for everything. If you come to my apartment I'll give you the money right now. Just tell me how much you think that jewelry was worth and—"

"The money doesn't matter," she said. "It was the sentimental value."

"Jesus, you don't know how sorry I am about all this," I said. "Just tell me the amount—any amount and I'll give you the money. Please—it's important that I do this."

"I have no idea what it was worth."

"Give me a ballpark figure."

"I don't know—maybe a few hundred dollars."

"No problem," I said. "I'll give you the money right now—three hundred for the jewelry and the hundred I owe you—but you have to promise not to talk to my boss or the police."

"Do you have the money with you?"

"Wait one second," I said.

I went back into the bar and asked Frank if he could cover for me for about fifteen minutes, a half hour tops. He said it was no problem and I came back out wearing my leather coat.

"Where are we going?" Janene asked.

"To give you your money."

"I thought you had it with you."

"No, it's in my apartment."

"I don't want to go to your apartment."

"Why not?"

"Why don't you just send me the money?"

"Put cash in the mail? Come on, it'll take two minutes. I really want to make up for what I did to you."

She looked away, trying to make up her mind, then she looked back at me and said, "All right, let's go."

It was weird walking next to her. She had her arms crossed in front of her chest and she didn't say a word. I didn't say anything either. I was pissed at her for threatening to call the cops. After what Rodrigo pulled in the kitchen, I was getting sick of people trying to blackmail me.

We turned on to Sixty-fourth Street. When we got to my building, I headed up the stoop, but Janene stopped on the sidewalk.

"You coming up?"

"No," she said, "I think I'll just wait out here."

"Come on, it's freezing out."

"It's okay," she said.

"What? You don't trust me?"

"I just feel like waiting down here on the street."

There was a group of teenagers across the street, smoking cigarettes and laughing.

"Whatever," I said.

I went upstairs and came back down with the four hundred dollars. She put the money away in her coat pocket.

"I really hope you quit gambling," she said, "for your own sake."

I watched her walk away toward York Avenue, hoping she was out of my life for good.

Twelve

Walking home after work, I didn't feel like being alone. Remembering how Susan Lepidus had asked me to call her sometime, I stopped at the nearest phone booth. The phone rang four times and then her answering machine picked up. I was about to hang up when she said, "Wait—hold on," then she turned off the machine and, sounding tired, said, "Hello."

I realized that one-thirty was probably kind of late to call somebody.

"Hey, Susan," I said, "it's Tommy. You know, from O'Reilley's."

She didn't say anything for a few seconds then she said, "Oh, hi, how are you?"

"Hope I didn't wake you," I said.

"No…I mean I was just getting into bed…what time is it?"

"About one-thirty," I said. "I just got off work. I know it's late to be calling, but I want you to know it was really nice seeing you again the other night. I've been thinking about you a lot since then."

"That's sweet. It was nice seeing you again too."

"I know this is short notice, but I figured I'd be spontaneous. You want to go out for a late drink?"

"Now?"

"Why not? There are a few places still open."

"I don't know," she said. "I mean I have to go to work tomorrow."

"That's right," I said. "I always forget how normal people work in the *morning*."

She laughed.

"Maybe we could go out some other time," I said. "Unless...nah, that's a stupid idea."

"What is?"

"I was thinking, I could come by your place, if you want. Just to say hi, have a quick drink and leave."

"I don't know," she said.

"Forget about it then," I said. "I told you it was a stupid idea. I'll call you some other time. I'm off on Tuesdays. Maybe tomorrow night we can do something."

"I have plans tomorrow."

"Some other time then."

"Wait," she said. "I guess you could come over now."

"You sure?"

"Yeah...why not? Do you remember where I live?"

"I sure do," I said. "Should I bring over some beer?"

"That's all right, I have some in the fridge."

"See you in a few."

I started to walk, but my feet were cold in my motorcycle boots, so I jogged up First Avenue with the stiff wind in my face. Susan lived on Eighty-third Street between Third and Lex. It was about twenty blocks from the phone booth, but it only took me about ten minutes to get there.

I'd walked Susan home that night after we went out

dancing, but I'd never been up to her apartment. It was a doorman building, but not nearly as nice as Frank's. The doorman buzzed her and I took the elevator up.

Susan looked good, especially for two in the morning. She was wearing jeans and a long black T-shirt and she'd put on makeup—lipstick and blush.

After I kissed her hello on the cheek, she invited me into the apartment. It was a small place—bigger than my dump, but so was just about every other apartment in the city. It had an L-shape with a little kitchen and a living room in the big part, and the bedroom area was off to the right. A U2 poster was hanging on the wall above the couch.

She took my coat and put it on the back of a chair.

"Why don't you sit down?" she said.

She pointed toward a seat at the kitchen table.

"That's all right," I said. "So this is a nice little place you got here."

"Thanks," she said, twirling a few long strands of her curly red hair with a finger. "Can I get you a beer or something?"

"Why not?" I said.

She went to the fridge, took out two Heinekens, and put them down on the counter.

"I'm really glad you called me," she said, opening the beer. "I was hoping you would."

"I should've called you right away," I said.

"It's all right," she said.

"No, it isn't," I said. "I told you I'd call you and I never did. That was wrong."

"It's all right," she said. "It's just as much my fault as it was yours. I could've called you too."

I put my hands against her hips and turned her around toward me. I kissed her—gently at first, then I pushed her back against the refrigerator, kissing her all over her face. She was kissing me back, sucking on my earlobes. As I was unhooking her bra she said, "Wait, you really think we should do this?"

"Yes," I said. "Unless you don't want to."

Her bra fell onto the floor and she pulled off my shirt. I carried her to the bed, still kissing her, when the doorbell rang.

Susan looked terrified.

"Who the hell could that be?" I said.

"I don't know," she said.

"So let's just ignore it," I said.

"We can't."

"Why not?"

"Because he knows I'm home."

"Who knows?"

"My boyfriend."

"You have a boyfriend?"

"Ex-boyfriend. The guy I was at the bar with the other night."

The knocking was louder now. Then the guy—I remembered his name was Jim—said, "Come on, Susan, open up! Open the fuckin' door, Susan!"

"Just forget about it," I whispered. "He'll go away."

"No, he sounds drunk," Susan said. "He'll wake the whole building. Why did my stupid doorman let him up?"

"Susan!" Jim yelled. "Open the door Susan! Open the fucking door!"

"I'll go talk to him," Susan said.

She put her shirt on.

"You sure?" I said.

"Yeah, it'll be fine. Wait one sec."

Susan went to the door and I was thinking how, when she came back, I'd make up some excuse and go home. Although Susan was a nice girl and she was very good looking, we didn't have anything in common and I couldn't remember why I'd called her in the first place.

Susan and Jim were talking at the door.

"Come on, lemme in," Jim said.

"I'll call you tomorrow," Susan said.

"No, let me in now," Jim said. "I wanna talk to you."

"It's too late," Susan said.

"Why, you got someone here?"

"Nobody's here."

"Who's here?"

"No one."

"Stop it…Jim!"

Jim pushed his way into the apartment. He stormed into the bedroom area and saw me sitting there on Susan's bed without a shirt on. He was wearing a business suit, his tie partially unwound. His hair was a mess and he looked drunk.

For a few seconds, he just stood there, shocked, then he said, "What the fuck is this shit?"

"Just go home," Susan said. "I'll call you tomorrow."

"You fuckin' son of a bitch," Jim said to me.

He stood there for another second or two, then he charged me. I stood up and pushed him away, which wasn't very hard. The guy was about five-six and probably weighed eighty pounds less than me.

Susan was screaming for Jim to go home and I said, "Just take it easy—take it easy, all right? I don't wanna hurt you, just take it easy."

"Fuck you," Jim said, spraying spit. "Just fuck you."

He tried to punch me in the face and missed by about a foot. Then he came at me again and grabbed my chain with the little gold barbell. The chain snapped and the barbell fell onto the floor.

"Look what you did," I said. "Look what you did."

"Fuck you," Jim said.

I went after him, punching him in the face again and again. His nose started gushing blood, then he fell onto the floor, curled up into a ball, yelling, "Help me, Susan! Help me!"

Finally, Susan pulled me away. She kneeled next to Jim and said to me, "What's wrong with you? Why wouldn't you stop?"

I picked up my barbell chain, happy to see that only the clasp was broken.

"Just get the hell out of here," Susan said to me. "Leave!"

I put on my shirt and coat and left the apartment. Walking home down Third Avenue, I finally started to calm down.

When I arrived at my place, I went right into the bathroom and washed up. I didn't even have a scratch on my face, but my knuckles were sore. I felt bad for hitting Jim as hard as I did and I hoped he wasn't seriously hurt.

I put the barbell and the busted chain away in my dresser drawer, then I sat at the table and counted the money I had left over from the robbery. The total came to about $1,700 and tomorrow was my day off. Maybe what I needed was to get away for a day or two—clear my head.

Then, just like that, I drove out to La Guardia Airport and hopped the next flight to Vegas.

It was last-minute notice so they charged me through the eyeballs for a ticket. I paid eight hundred bucks for the round-trip flight, when it probably would have cost me half that much if I bought the ticket in advance or took one of those gambling junkets. Now I only had about four hundred bucks on me—I'd left five hundred at home—so if I didn't hit something right away it was going to be a short trip.

The plane took off at around 6:30 in the morning. I switched planes in Detroit and arrived in Vegas at eleven o'clock, ready to rock and roll. I didn't sleep a wink the whole flight, but I was wide awake anyway.

I took a cab to the strip, shocked how big the place was. For years people had been telling me, "You gotta see Vegas to believe it," and now I knew what they meant.

I didn't know where to go first so I had the cab driver drop me off at Bally's. Sticking to the plan I'd made on the plane, I went to the first roulette wheel I saw and let three hundred bucks ride on black. The ball spun around, bounced out of a red slot, and landed in black. I let the six hundred ride and black came in again. I'd just won a free trip to Vegas.

At a blackjack table my hot streak continued. After about ten minutes I was up over a grand. I could do no wrong—splitting nines and pulling aces, hitting on fifteen and sixteen and pulling fives and sixes, sticking with single digits and watching the dealer bust. I tipped the dealer fifty bucks for his trouble and headed over to the racebook.

I bet on a couple of simulcast races from New York and Florida. I lost at Calder, but I hit an exacta and win bet at Aqueduct that put me up another G. I played slots for a while, breaking even, then I hit the blackjack tables again, winning another five hundred bucks. I had been in the casino for about an hour and a half and I was up about three grand. I was going to head over to another casino, maybe pick up a bite to eat, when I saw this blonde smiling at me.

I knew right away she was a pro, sizing me up as a john. Her lips were painted with bright pink fluorescent lipstick and she was fluttering her long eyelashes. She had a big curvy shape in a silver sequined dress. Maybe this was exactly what I needed—some nice, uncomplicated sex. I went over to her and asked her what she charged. She said two hundred an hour. I told her I'd meet her in the lobby outside the casino in ten minutes.

I cashed in my chips and rented a room. The hooker was waiting where she said she'd be and she was looking better and better.

In the elevator she asked me if I'd been to Vegas before and I said, "No, it's my first time," and she said, "So how do you like it so far?" I said, "Not too bad." We didn't say anything else to each other until we got to the room. Then, as soon as the door closed, she said, "So where do you want me?"

We did it once, fast, then I took my time. When we were through, I gave her that two hundred bucks, plus a fifty-dollar tip.

"Thanks," she said. "That's so sweet of you."

She invited me to watch her "perform" later at some strip bar at the other end of town, but I told her I doubted I'd be able to make it.

A few minutes after she left the room, I went back down to the casino.

I wolfed down a couple of burgers at one of the hotel's restaurants using a comp card, then I was ready for more action. I was planning to leave for New York early tomorrow morning and go to work tomorrow night. I probably could've used some rest, but there was no way I was going to miss out on any gambling time in Vegas—especially since I had about $2,600 burning a hole in my pocket.

I wanted to check out as many casinos as I could so I went across the street to The Flamingo. I bought two thousand bucks in chips and went right to a craps table, blowing a grand in fifteen minutes. Before things got really out of control, I got up and started playing blackjack again. I didn't like the dealer at the table I was sitting at—he was smiling and joking around too much—so I walked around and found a

table with an empty seat in the anchor slot. My chip
pile was shrinking, but I guess my jet lag was starting
to catch up with me because I was too tired to walk
around anymore. So I stayed at the table and eventually I started to win again. After about two hours, I
won back the grand I'd lost at craps, plus another
seven hundred. I cashed in my chips and took my
comp card and headed toward the restaurant, ready to
pig out on a steak-and-potatoes dinner.

"Looking for a date, honey?"

I'd just left the casino when I looked over and saw
the best-looking hooker I'd ever seen. She had long
brown hair and she was wearing a tight black dress.

"How much?" I asked.

"Five for an hour you won't forget."

I guess I could've brought her to my room at Bally's,
but I was so tired I didn't want to waste the energy
crossing the street. Besides, I was rolling in dough so I
just rented a two-hundred-dollar room at the Flamingo
and took the hooker upstairs with me. I knew I wouldn't
be able to get in two goes this time, but I got my
money's worth anyway.

Later on, I could barely get out of bed and I had to
pace around my room for about fifteen minutes before
I could make it downstairs. Two rare steaks and a side
order of shrimp pumped me up enough to make it into
a cab and head crosstown to Caesar's Palace for some
poker action. Forty-five minutes later I was broke.

I still don't know how I managed to lose all my
money so fast. It probably had something to do with
being the worst poker player in the world and sitting

down at a high-stakes table with blue balls on zero
sleep. All I remember clearly is sitting across from two
guys in cowboy hats, and next thing I knew I was sitting on a chair in the lobby with my head in my hands.

I only had about forty dollars left on me—enough
to get a cab to the airport and to pay to pick up my car
from the airport parking lot in New York. I thought
about going back to one of my hotel rooms, but I knew
there was no way I'd fall asleep so I decided to just
head out to the terminal and wait for my flight tomorrow morning. I sat down near my gate, so tired I
was dizzy. I noticed that people kept sitting down next
to me then getting up and moving away. Then I remembered how the cab driver had opened all the windows
and how people at the poker table had been giving me
funny looks. I hadn't showered since Monday morning
—over two days ago—and I probably smelled as bad
as Pete Logan.

I probably looked like shit too. I needed a shave and
I was wearing the same outfit—jeans and a black sweatshirt with my black leather coat—that I'd left New
York in. I had about five hours until my flight left but I
couldn't grab any shut-eye.

Finally, at around six in the morning my flight
boarded. I was hoping to catch some Zs on the plane,
but I couldn't sleep. I was staring out the window, at
some clouds, when I saw my father on the wing and
my mother was next to him. They were both laughing,
then my father pushed me and I was tumbling down a
flight of stairs, screaming, trying to stop, but I was
falling faster and faster.

"Excuse me, sir...sir?"

I looked up at the stewardess leaning over me.

"Sorry to wake you, but the pilot has put on the fasten seat belt sign."

"Thanks," I said, looking out the window, scratching the scar on the back of my head.

It was snowing in New York. It wasn't coming down hard, but there were a few inches on the ground. I was so exhausted I thought I was going to pass out, but I somehow made it out to the parking lot. I brushed the snow off the windshield and the back windows with my hands, then I got into the car. Naturally, the piece of shit wouldn't start. I asked the parking attendant for a boost and then I had to stand outside waiting for an hour, freezing my ass off. I was almost ready to just leave my car there, take the license off and ditch it. But then they got the car started and, going about thirty miles per hour the whole way, I made it into the city about an hour and a half later.

It was around three in the afternoon—an impossible time to find a parking space in Manhattan. After driving around for about twenty minutes, I gave up and left the car in front of a hydrant on my block. Let the cops tow the dung heap away—do me a favor.

Walking up the stairs in my building, I felt like I was climbing the Statue of Liberty. In my apartment, I went right to my couch, not even bothering to open the bed. Then I heard a funny squeaking sound. I thought it was the pipes or something so I tried to ignore it. But it was too damn annoying so I got up to find out where the noise was coming from. It sounded like it was coming from the kitchen sink, maybe inside the pipes, then I looked down and saw the little mouse caught in a glue trap. I picked up the trap with the mouse stuck on it, opened the window, and flung it across the street like a frisbee.

Back on the couch, I started to dream. I was in the winner's circle at Hollywood Park. My horse had just won a big race and Jack Nicholson and Robert Redford and Al Pacino were there, shaking my hand. Then an alarm went off and people started running and yelling, "Fire! Fire!" and I looked over and my horse was dead. I tried to run away, but I was stuck to a giant glue trap. I woke up, sweating, wondering why the noise wouldn't stop. Then I realized what was going on. My fucking phone was ringing.

Thirteen

"Tommy? I didn't wake you, did I?"

The voice sounded like somebody I knew, but I was so spaced it took a second or two before I matched it with a name—Debbie O'Reilley.

"No," I said, wondering why the hell I didn't just let my answering machine pick up. "What's going on?"

"I should be asking you that question. I've been trying to hunt you down for two days now. Either you've been screening your calls or you went away without telling me. Either way I'm very upset with you."

As usual, she sounded drunk.

"I was in Vegas," I said.

"Vegas? *Las* Vegas?"

"You calling me for any reason, because I was about to go to sleep."

"Sleep? Don't you have to work tonight?"

Shit, I forgot all about work. There was no way in hell I was going in feeling like this.

"I'm calling in sick," I said.

"Really? Well, that's convenient—and timely too. Because I'm feeling kind of lonely and I was hoping I could come over to visit."

"What's that?"

"I said I want to come over to your place."

"Here?"

"Why not? You're not trying to avoid me, are you?"

I was starting to fall asleep again.

"Look, I really gotta hang up now."

"I'm coming over—I just got your address from Information."

"Don't come here," I said, waking up. "I'm serious."

"Why? You're too tired? It's all right—I'll take a nap with you."

"Wait," I said. I remembered that Frank had hired a detective.

"Don't come here," I said. "That's a shitty idea."

"Don't you want to see me again?" she said, trying to sound sexy.

"It's just not a good time right now," I said. "Trust me, all right?"

"I really want to see you again, Tommy. I don't know what I did to upset you so much, but I promise I won't do it again."

"Maybe some other time," I said. "I'm really not feeling too good right now."

"Poor thing," she said. "Are you sick? Should I bring you over some chicken soup?"

"No, the thing is there's a detective watching you," I said. "Frank told me about it the other day—"

"Oh, *that's* why you're so worried. You don't have to worry about that, darling. That slob was following me around all day yesterday and I had no problem losing him. Don't worry about anything. I'll be right there."

"Come on, Debbie, don't—"

She hung up. I said "hello" a couple of times then I put the receiver down, still feeling dazed. I closed my eyes, trying to go back to Hollywood Park, but I must've fallen asleep without dreaming because it seemed like a second later the buzzer was ringing. I got up to answer it, forgetting where I was. Then I heard Debbie's voice on the intercom. Now I was really getting pissed off. Why the hell couldn't she take no for an answer?

I buzzed her up, hoping the detective didn't follow her. No matter what, I was going to tell her to get the hell away from me and to stay away.

She was wearing a fur coat and black boots. Her fake blond hair was done up like Ivana Trump and she had a load of makeup on. She looked better than she did the other day at her apartment, but she still disgusted me.

I noticed she was holding a white plastic shopping bag.

"It was quite a climb to get up here," she said. "I can't believe people actually *live* in these buildings."

She moved in to kiss me with her glossy lips and I was too tired to turn my head. I picked up the Scotch odor right away. Then she backed away, making a face like she just stepped into a big pile of dog shit.

"What's that smell?"

"Me," I said.

"My God, you're filthy…what *happened* to you?"

"I told you, I was in Vegas."

"Don't they have showers in Las Vegas?"

"Why did you have to come over here?" I said. "Why couldn't you listen to me?"

"Because I was lonely and I wanted to see you. Aren't you happy to see me?"

"This was really stupid," I said. "If that detective—"

"You don't have to worry about *him*," she said. "I saw that slob following me again when I left my building. I found a police officer on the corner and told him that a man was following me, then I got in a cab and came over here. Oh, but first I stopped at a Chinese restaurant and bought you a couple of containers of hot-and-sour soup. It always does wonders for me when I feel a cold coming on."

"How do you know he didn't follow you out of the restaurant?" I said. "Maybe you just didn't see him."

"My God, will you stop being so paranoid? The way you're talking you'd think you *did* have something to hide."

She passed by me and went toward the kitchen counter. I closed the door and bolted it.

"I hate to be so blunt," she said, "but you really could use a shower *and* a maid."

"If you don't like the way I smell, there's the door."

She thought about it a second then said, "No, actually I'm starting to like the way you smell. You smell raw. It kind of turns me on." She put the shopping bag down on the counter. "Now I have a surprise for you so close your eyes."

I just stood there.

"You're no fun. Come on, play the game."

I crossed my arms in front of my chest.

"All right, but it won't be nearly as shocking."

She opened her coat and, except for her shiny black boots, she was buck naked.

"Get out of here," I said. I was looking away, trying not to see any more. "I'm serious."

"Well, *that* wasn't exactly the response I was expecting."

She came up to me and put her arms around my waist, rubbing against me, then she kissed me on the lips. I pushed her away.

"Just put your coat on and get out of here."

She took a few steps back. She was shaking a little bit too, maybe because she was so drunk.

"I only came here because I thought you wanted to see me," she said. "Because I thought we—"

"Look, whatever happened the other day, let's just forget about it, all right?"

"What's the matter, you didn't have a good time?"

"No."

"I don't think this is any way for you to treat your future wife."

"Excuse me? What the hell are you talking about?"

"Frank wants a divorce. He wanted to make an out-of-court settlement with me. At first, I was thinking about trying to milk him for all he was worth, but now I'm thinking about just accepting it. He said something about how he wants to move to Arizona, open a bar there. If I accept the settlement I'll get the apartment and enough money to live on comfortably, or for *us* to live on comfortably."

"How the hell did you get the idea I'd want to marry you?" I said.

"Why wouldn't you? Not only would you be getting

a woman who'd pleasure you like no woman could, but with Frank's money you'd never have to work again."

I started to laugh. I couldn't help it—it was just so damn funny.

"Why are you laughing?"

"Believe me," I said, "if you were me, you'd be laughing too."

"I really don't think you should be treating me this way. I might leave here very angry at you and then there's no telling what I might do. Maybe I'll just tell everybody about your dirty little secret."

"What do you mean?"

I wasn't laughing anymore.

"You know exactly what I mean."

"I have no idea what you're talking about," I said.

"I saw you the other night—stealing that money."

I stared at her, trying to figure out if she was lying.

"I think you're drunk and you should go home," I said.

"I was on my way to the bar to look for Frank and I saw you," she said, "walking home with that garbage bag. I was wondering why you were taking garbage home from work with you, but the next day it all made sense."

"You're full of shit," I said, but I knew she was telling the truth. There was no other way she could've known about the garbage bag unless Rodrigo had told her, and I didn't see why he would have.

"It's too bad," she said. "We could've had a good life together."

"You're wrong," I said. "I didn't take that money."

"Oh really? Then what's that?"

She was looking toward the kitchen table where the money left over from the robbery—five hundred dollars, in twenties and fifties—was spread out.

"I bet you gambled the rest of it away in Las Vegas," she said.

She was buttoning up her coat.

"Where are you going?"

"Where do you think I'm going? Obviously, you don't want me here."

"Hold up a second," I said. "Come on—stay. I was just so tired from my trip I didn't know what I was saying before."

"I think you're lying."

"I'm serious," I said. I opened the buttons of her coat and pulled her toward me. I smelled the Scotch on her breath. "I don't want you to go—I'm glad you're here. Why wouldn't I be glad? You just can't believe the shit I've been through the past couple days. Driving back from the airport I thought I was gonna pass out at the wheel. Come on, stay. I want you here. That's the real truth."

I kissed her hard, swirling my tongue around in her one-hundred-proof mouth.

After a while I pulled back and said, "So what do you say?"

"I don't know. A second ago you sounded like you were really mad at me, like you *hated* me—"

"Forget about that. I'm telling you, I really didn't know what the hell I was saying. If you wanna know the truth, I was pretty excited when I heard you and

Frank were splitting up. I'm tired of being single, struggling, waking up alone every day. I'm getting to the age where I want to settle down."

She held onto the edge of the table, trying to keep her balance.

"You know what I think?" she said. "I think you're just saying all this to shut me up because you're afraid I'm gonna call the police."

"No, I'm saying this because I want you to get into bed with me."

I took off her coat completely and let it fall onto the floor. I started kissing her again.

"Tommy, can I ask you one more thing?"

"Shoot," I said.

"Before, when you laughed about us getting married, you didn't really—"

"Of course not," I said.

"—because I didn't mean it the way I sounded. I guess I've just been drinking and...I mean that's what I'd like to happen someday, but it doesn't mean it has to happen right away...I mean we can let it happen naturally and—"

"Forget about it," I said.

She smiled.

I kissed her some more, then she said, "Do you have anything to drink in this apartment?"

"There's beer in the fridge," I said. "Help yourself."

While she went to get a beer, I went into the bathroom. Standing over the bowl, I felt like the floor was moving and I had to hold on to the shower door to keep my balance. Then I caught another whiff of myself. I smelled so bad I didn't know how Debbie could stand to be in the same room with me.

When I came out of the bathroom, Debbie had pulled open the couch. She was lying on her back naked. I turned out the light. It wasn't totally dark outside yet so I could still see the outline of her body. I didn't know how I was going to go through with this. I got into bed and climbed on top of her. I was holding her down with my arms, taking it nice and slow at first, then speeding up. She started to moan and then I decided to just get it over with. I picked up a pillow and pressed it down over her face. She fought back awhile, kicking and swinging her arms like a maniac, but I kept pushing down. Finally, she stopped squirming.

I turned on the light and lifted the pillow slowly. Her mouth was halfway open and her glassy brown eyes were looking at the ceiling.

I got out of bed quickly. I started pacing my apartment, deciding what to do next. I knew I had to figure out a way to get rid of her body. It was probably stupid to put that pillow over her face without thinking it through first, but what choice did I have?

Sitting down again, I started to doze off next to her and I knew this was a bad idea. I couldn't go to sleep now—what if Debbie was wrong and that detective *had* followed her to my apartment? He could be outside right now, waiting for her to leave.

I stood up out of bed and went to the kitchen sink and splashed my face with ice-cold water. Then I leaned out the window, looking for the detective. But I just saw a couple of people, on their way home from work, and a black guy across the street, looking in garbage cans.

I had to come up with a plan. I was shooting blanks, then, thinking harder, I decided that I had to get the body into my car somehow and dump it someplace outside of Manhattan. But there was no way I could do that now, with so many people around. I'd have to wait until the middle of the night—midnight at least. In the meantime, I'd just have to hope that detective wasn't watching me.

It was twenty past five. I decided to go into work tonight after all. I had to act like it was a normal night. If the cops came around asking questions I'd have to be able to explain where I was all night. Besides, I knew that if I went to sleep now there was no way I was getting up in a few hours.

I took a shower. It felt good, getting clean again, but I was afraid I was going to pass out and I held onto the soap rack the whole time.

It seemed like a bad idea to leave the body just lying there, so I covered it with a blanket and then I piled up the couch cushions on top.

I finished getting ready for work, putting on my usual jeans, black crew-neck, and motorcycle boots, but I missed my gold barbell chain. I realized I was starving and then I saw the two containers of hot-and-sour soup that Debbie had brought over for me. I drank the lukewarm soup straight from the containers, then I put on my leather coat and left the apartment.

Outside my building, I looked around, but there didn't seem to be anybody watching me. There were still some flurries coming down, but the snow was pretty much gone from the sidewalks. It was getting cold again—the wind whipping down First Avenue like a motherfucker—and I missed the eighty or whatever the hell degrees it was in Las Vegas.

I was glad it was a Wednesday night and the weather was bad because the last thing I felt like doing tonight was checking a lot of IDs. Gary was supposed to work tonight, but Gil was behind the bar, so I figured Gary was still pissed off at Frank or maybe he had quit for good

"Hey," I said to Gil.

"How's it going, Tommy?"

Gil didn't look up from his book when he was talking to me. There were about ten people in the bar and a reggae CD was playing on the stereo.

"Frank around?" I asked.

"He went out for a second. He'll be right back."

I went to hang up my coat. Kathy came by with a tray of mozzarella sticks.

"Hey, how's it going, Kath?"

"Fine," she said, walking past me.

I was still hungry, but I didn't feel like dealing with Rodrigo in the kitchen. I figured I'd just order a pizza or something later on. When I came back out front, Frank was just coming into the bar.

"What's this?" he said. "You growing a beard?"

"Maybe," I said. "Like it?"

"It's okay." He looked at me closer. "You feeling okay?"

"I just didn't get too much sleep last night."

"It's gonna be a slow night. If you want, you can go home. Gil's gonna take off soon, but Kathy can cover the bar."

"It's all right," I said.

Frank went to the back. The room was starting to spin and I felt like I was going to pass out for real. Without my coat on, I jogged down the block to the Korean deli. I bought a large coffee, a couple of those little carrot cakes, two Snickers bars, and two packs of Starburst. I figured that filling myself up with sugar and caffeine might be the only thing to keep me awake.

When I got back to the bar Frank was sitting at a table across from a fat man with curly brown hair. I'd never seen the guy before, but I knew right away that he was the detective Frank had hired.

The guy was wearing a big black winter jacket, jeans, and work boots. He looked over at me for a second, then he looked back at Frank. Over the reggae music, I couldn't hear everything he was saying, although a couple of times I heard him say "Debbie." But I wasn't worried. If the detective saw Debbie going into my apartment today, he would have come to talk to me by now. I sat down at the bar with my coffee and opened one of the carrot cakes. Looking straight ahead, I was watching Frank and the detective in the mirror behind the bar, and there was a break in the music so I picked up on more of their conversation.

"Yeah, I'm sure," the detective was saying. "I went back to the building and the doorman said he didn't see her go in. I hung out awhile, for maybe an hour, but she didn't come back."

"Well, what can you do?" Frank said. "You'll just have to try again tomorrow."

"Don't worry, I'll catch her," the detective said. "I just need another day or two and tomorrow I'm gonna wear a disguise so she won't see me."

"Do whatever you have to do," Frank said.

After they bullshitted for a little while longer, Frank and the detective stood up and shook hands. Then the detective left the bar without looking in my direction. Frank came over and sat down on the stool next to me.

"That was the guy I told you I hired to follow Debbie."

"He find anything out?"

"He saw her leaving the building this afternoon, probably on her way to meet one of her lover boys, when she stopped and told a cop that some guy was following her. So the cop stopped Fred—that's his name—and by the time Fred explained what was going on, Debbie was gone—in a cab."

"That really sucks Easter eggs, huh?" I said.

"I just hope this guy Fred knows what he's doing— Gil, lemme get one on the rocks—I mean he's a professional so he should know."

"I don't think you gotta worry," I said. "Knowing the way Debbie gets around I bet he'll get some good pictures for you to use in no time."

Now Frank was staring off. I realized I'd probably said the wrong thing.

"Sorry," I said. "I didn't mean—"

"No, it's all right. You're just telling the goddamn truth."

Gil put down Frank's drink. Frank took a long sip then said, "You're gonna think I'm crazy, but in a way I still love her. Pretty pathetic, huh?"

"No, I understand," I said. "I mean she's your wife, you share the same bed…"

"I know you're right," Frank said. "You've always been right, giving me good advice, but I never had the sense to listen to you. The shrinks have a name for what I'm talking about—Jesus, I swear, my fuckin' mind's going."

"But you know what I think?" I said. "I think once she's out of the picture you'll forget all about her. You'll be out there in Arizona with all those beautiful women—you'll find somebody who'll treat you a lot better than Debbie ever did."

"You ever seen me in swimming trunks? It's not a pretty sight."

"Come on, I'm sure you look great," I said. "And a guy like you, from New York, you'll have no problem at all."

"No, I think Debbie was the best I'll ever get."

"You gotta be kiddin' me. What you gotta do is start moving up. I'm serious. Instead of looking for women in their forties, look for women in their fifties and sixties, maybe even in their seventies. Arizona's like Florida. They got all those rich widows down there, waiting for a guy to come along. And once you get that bar going, forget about it—you'll have a woman for every night of the week."

"Co-dependent," Frank said.

"What?"

"That's the word I was thinking of before—I'm co-dependent. I like to be with sick, fucked-up women because I'm sick and fucked up myself. I never told you this before, but my first wife was an alcoholic too. She wasn't as bad as Debbie, but she was close. My point is maybe the problem's me, not her—maybe any woman would run around on me. Maybe I should call off the divorce and try to patch things up."

"I don't think that would be a good idea."

"Why not? You know, most of the problems we have are all because of booze. If I could just get her to lay off, maybe we could go get some counseling, try to work things out—"

"You're not serious, I hope."

"No, I wish I was, but I know it's too late. I'll go through with the goddamn divorce, go out to cactus country and see what life has in store for me. But I'm telling you—I don't think anything I find out there'll be better than what I have in front of me right now."

Frank took another swig of his vodka-tonic. I stood up and stretched.

"So I guess Gary's not coming in tonight, huh?" I said.

"Haven't seen or heard from him since Monday," Frank said. "His tape picks up when I call—for all I know he left New York. But I'll tell you one thing— I'm glad you're taking over the bar instead of him. The damn kid is just too unreliable. I need somebody running this bar I can trust."

"You can trust me."

"I know I can. You're probably the only person in the world I can trust right now. Jesus, you look like you're about to fall down. Why don't you go home?"

"That's all right," I said. "I'm fine."

"No, I'm serious. I mean I appreciate you coming in here when you're feeling like this, but it's gonna be a slow night—Gil can proof at the bar—"

"Forget about it," I said, patting Frank on the back.

I went into the bathroom and passed out. I came to a few seconds later with a nice bruise on my ass. I splashed cold water on my face.

Eating the Snickers bar and the second carrot cake gave me a boost. I was hoping it would be a slow night, but some fuckin' kid picked tonight of all nights to celebrate his twenty-first birthday and he had to do it at O'Reilley's. College kids were spilling in all night—most of them looked eighteen or nineteen, and some looked younger, but I was too tired to do my job right. I just sat on my stool, waving everybody in, even a kid with a bogus Jersey license that looked like it was made on a computer.

I drank a couple of Cokes to keep the caffeine coming, but at around 11:30 I couldn't take it anymore. I told Frank I was taking off and I headed down First Avenue.

The wind had picked up and the temperature must have dropped another ten degrees. It was probably in the teens now, heading down into the single digits. My hands and feet were frozen stiff and it felt like I had icicles on my face. I was starting to get a sore throat.

I was turning the corner onto my block when I realized what deep shit I could be in. This afternoon I'd parked my car in front of a hydrant. If the cops towed it away I didn't know how I'd get rid of the body.

I jogged up the block and thank God the car was still there. It was like a fuckin' miracle—I didn't even get a ticket.

Amazingly, the engine caught on the first try. I drove up the block and double-parked in front of my building. Leaving the engine running, I went inside. I was dizzy, going up the stairs. In my apartment, I spread the blanket down on the floor and then I lifted Debbie up. She was already stiff and purple, but for some reason her body was warm. I was about to get the pillow to finish her off, when I realized that she only felt warm because my hands were so fucking freezing.

I let out a deep breath and smiled, thinking this would all seem very funny someday.

I laid Debbie down on the blanket. I put the fur coat back on her and then I put her pocketbook over her shoulder. I looked around to make sure she hadn't brought anything else into the apartment with her. All I noticed was the shopping bag from the Chinese restaurant, but I figured I'd get rid of that later. I rolled Debbie up in the blanket.

Normally, I could've carried her down to the street, no problem, but I was so tired it felt like she was twice her actual weight. On the second floor, I thought I heard somebody coming out of their apartment. I froze, but the noise stopped.

When I got down to the vestibule there was a man

passing by outside, but he was looking straight ahead and didn't see me. I waited until he was down the block and there were no cars passing by and then I carried Debbie outside. Thanks to the cold, there weren't any other people on the street. Moving fast, I opened the trunk. I had a lot of shit in there—a spare tire, tools, old clothes—but I couldn't start cleaning now. I stuffed her inside. Part of her body wouldn't fit so I had to bend it. But part of her must've still been blocking something because I still couldn't close the fucking thing. I tried a few more times and then, finally, using all my might, I slammed the trunk down and it locked.

I got on the FDR Drive, heading downtown. I took the Manhattan Bridge and stayed on Flatbush. The Brooklyn streets were empty and if I could've gotten my car going over twenty-five miles an hour I might've made every light. As it was, it was stop-and-go like I was in rush-hour traffic. A couple of times I caught myself dozing at the wheel and I fought to stay awake. I figured that some loud music would help keep me up so I turned on the radio to a rap station and cranked the volume.

I was driving past Church Avenue when I spotted the police car behind me. Then the siren came on and the cop came on the bullhorn and told me to pull over.

I figured there was probably just something wrong with my car—maybe one of my taillights was out or something. No matter what, I had to stay cool. The police car stopped behind me with the brights shining in my rear-view mirror.

A cop came up to my window. He was a white guy, about my size and age. He had a mustache.

"Hey, how's it goin'?" I said.

"Can you turn that music down please?"

I lowered the volume, realizing that with the way that rap music was blasting they must've thought they were pulling over a drug dealer.

"Can I see your license and registration please?"

I took my license out of my wallet and the registration out of the glove compartment and handed them to him. "What's the problem?" I said. "I know I couldn't've been speeding—not in this piece of shit."

I laughed, hoping he'd laugh too but he didn't. He took out a flashlight and shined it at my face.

"Your eyes are bloodshot. Have you been drinking tonight?"

"You kiddin' me? I'm exhausted. I'm just trying to get to my brother's house so I can get some rest."

He shined a flashlight into the car—looking on the floor in front of the front seat—then he checked out the back seat.

"Do you have any alcohol or drugs in the car?"

"No," I said.

"We were following you for a few blocks. Your car was swerving pretty badly."

"Sorry about that," I said. "It's just because I'm so tired. I just worked a twenty-hour shift at my job at the factory."

"Factory?"

"Yeah, I work at a watch factory down by the Navy Yards."

"You shouldn't be driving if you're exhausted."

"I wouldn't've, but it didn't hit me until a few minutes ago. But I got my second wind back now."

"Where does your brother live?"

"Avenue J."

He stared at me like he knew I was lying. I thought he was going to say "Get out of the car" and ask me to open the trunk. I had no idea what I'd do then, but instead he gave me back my license and registration and said, "Just be careful, pal."

I drove away, making sure I didn't swerve. The cop car followed me for a few more blocks and then it pulled over in front of a grocery store. I let out a long deep breath. The way my heart was pounding there was no way I was going to fall asleep at the wheel now.

I stayed on Flatbush for a couple more miles, then I made a right on Avenue U. When I got to Marine Park I made a U-turn and stopped by the curb under a busted lamppost. There were a few cars passing by and I made sure the coast was totally clear before I got out. I opened the trunk and took out the stiff body. Then, walking as fast as I could, I headed toward the marsh.

When I was a kid I used to go fishing in the Marine Park inlet. The water was so polluted I spent most of my time taking garbage off my hook and the only fish I brought home were the ones I found dead on the shore. The land before the shoreline wasn't as overrun by weeds as I remembered, but maybe this was because I was never there in the winter.

I walked in the darkness over the snow and mud. My feet were wet and cold, but I wanted to make sure

I was far enough away from the street before I put the body down. After walking for a little while longer, I was up to my ankles in freezing slush and I couldn't go any further. I dropped the body instead of putting it down, which turned out to be a big mistake. Slush splashed up all over me, including on my face. I was going to just walk away, but then I decided that it'd probably be a good idea to take the blanket with me. So I unrolled Debbie into the slush. She wound up on her back and at the same moment some clouds must've moved away from in front of the moon because, suddenly, there was pale blue light shining down on her white body.

If it was summer, the body would probably be discovered right away. But in the winter, in that mud and slush, they might not find her until March or April.

I got back into my car—first making sure nobody was around—then I drove away. On the off chance that the same cop car was still cruising Flatbush Avenue, I decided to take a different route home. I must've gotten my second wind, because I wasn't tired at all. I pulled into the parking lot of a supermarket on Coney Island Avenue and drove to the back where there was a dumpster. The supermarket was closed and the lot was empty. I got out of the car, tossed the muddy blanket into the dumpster, and drove away. Then I got on the Belt Parkway and headed back toward the city, chugging along in the right lane.

I still had mud all over me and I'd gotten the car dirty too.

Tomorrow I'd clean off my jeans and sneakers and

I'd clean the mud out of the car, although I probably didn't have to. Even if somebody did discover Debbie's body before the spring, nobody would ever suspect me.

Driving back to Manhattan my second wind was gone. I had to concentrate to stay awake, slapping myself in the face and wiggling my toes. Luckily, there was a spot right in front of my building that would be good until Friday morning at eleven o'clock.

I wobbled up the stairs to my apartment. I yanked the phone cord out of the wall and killed the lights. Then I collapsed onto my open bed and fell asleep as soon as my head hit the pillow.

Fourteen

When I woke up, it was almost noon. I plugged the phone into the wall, figuring I'd give Alan Schwartz a call. Just when I was about to dial, the phone rang.

"Can I speak to Tommy Russo please?"

"This is Tommy."

"Tommy—Alan Schwartz."

"This must be a sign of something," I said. "I was just picking up the phone to call you."

"I tried you earlier, but there was no answer," Alan said. "I have some very good news, great news really. Bill Tucker's going to try to claim a horse on Saturday. It's the one I mentioned the other day at the restaurant —Sunshine Brandy. We hope you can make it to the track."

"You kidding?" I said. "I'd have to be dead not to be there."

"Terrific," Alan said. "The only one who might not be able to make it is Steve, but he's going to try to get out of some Bar Mitzvah he has to go to. We're going to meet in the clubhouse, on the second floor near the escalator, before post time for the first race. I also wanted to apologize to you for the other day. I was wrapped up in this big project at work and I shouldn't've spoken to you the way I did. I hope there are no hard feelings."

"It was just a misunderstanding," I said. "I'm sorry too."

"Great," Alan said. "Anyway, I'm looking forward to seeing you there, Tommy. This should be a lot of fun."

Suddenly, I was in a great mood. I took a shower then pulled a pair of jeans out of the dirty laundry and put on a hooded sweatshirt. I shaved—only around my neck and my cheekbones. I liked my beard and I was planning to let it grow in all the way.

I was about to leave when I remembered my dirty clothes from last night. I didn't feel like doing laundry later so I put the muddy sneakers, jeans, and socks into a plastic bag and took it with me.

I took the 6 train downtown to Thirty-third Street and walked a few blocks crosstown. In a garbage can on the corner of Thirty-fourth and Seventh, I dumped the dirty clothes. I knew I couldn't go to the track on Saturday dressed like a slob—it was going to be my first day as a horse owner and I wanted to look the part—so I went up to the Macy's men's department and bought a two-hundred-dollar white suit and a nice black silk shirt, and then I went to the shoe department and bought a hundred-dollar pair of shiny black shoes. Now the money from the Super Bowl robbery was just about gone—I had another thirty bucks in my pocket and another sixty at home—but I wasn't worried. I knew there'd be a lot more where that came from.

On my way home, I stopped at a jewelry store and had my gold barbell chain repaired, then I went to

Smith & Wollensky on Third Avenue and had a burger with fries for lunch. Back at my apartment, I hung up my new clothes, and spent the rest of the afternoon on my couch, watching soap operas.

At around five-thirty I went to work. There was a pretty big Thursday night happy-hour crowd. Gil was working behind the bar so I figured Gary still wasn't coming to work. There were people at the bar, shouting orders, so I went to give Gil a hand. After I took a few orders and added a couple of dollars in tips to the tip jar, we finally had a chance to take a breather.

"Thanks a lot," Gil said. "It was starting to get crazy here."

We were listening to one of his shitty reggae CDs.

"You mind if I put in some Blondie?" I said.

"Go ahead," he said.

I put *Parallel Lines* in the CD player then I said to Gil, "So Gary's not coming in tonight, huh?"

"You didn't see the sign on the front of the bar?"

"What sign?"

"Frank's looking to hire a new night-time bartender. It looks like Gary's gone for good."

"You're kiddin' me?" I said. "That's too bad."

"I don't think so," Gil said. "I mean if the guy is really sick enough to steal money from his own father, who cares what happens to him?"

"Yeah, I guess that's true," I said. "But what I meant is it's too bad for Frank. It's just a fucked-up situation any way you look at it."

Gil and I took a few more drink orders and then the

crowd started to thin out. I was going to take a break,
maybe get something to eat in the kitchen, when two
cops came into the bar. They weren't the same cops
from the other day. One of them was a thin white guy,
about my height. The other guy was short, black and
heavy. I didn't have time to think about what was going
on. The black cop came right up to me at the bar and
said, "Is Frank O'Reilley here?"

"I don't know," I said. "Why? What's this all about?"

"It's personal business. We need to talk to Mr.
O'Reilley right away."

Gil came over. "Frank's in the office, in the back.
Just walk straight back and it's the first door on the
right."

"What do you think's going on?" Gil said to me.

"Probably just more about the robbery," I said.
"Maybe they found the guy who did it."

Gil went to take an order and I poured myself a
pint of Sam Adams. I chugged half of it, but it didn't
relax me. I was trying to think of all the reasons why
the cops could be here, except the one reason I didn't
want to think about. I hoped it had something to do
with the robbery, but if it had to do with Debbie maybe
it wasn't as bad as I thought. Maybe Frank had just
reported her missing. That would make sense, after
he woke up this morning and she wasn't in bed next
to him.

I started to feel better. There was no way they
could've found her so fast—not where I left her.

The cops returned from the back and left the bar

without looking over at me. They looked serious, like they'd just told a guy his wife was found dead in some half-frozen swampland in Brooklyn. Then Frank came from the back, crying like he was at a funeral, and I knew I was right.

He had his coat over his shoulder and he was heading toward the door. I went over to him, cutting him off.

"What's the matter?" I asked. "What's going on?"

He looked at me. His face was ugly and tears were streaming down his cheeks.

"She's dead!" he screamed. "She's fucking dead!"

Blondie was singing "Heart of Glass" and it was so loud in the bar that only the people who were standing close by were paying attention to us.

"Who?" I said.

"Debbie," he said crying. "I gotta get out of here."

"What do you mean, 'dead'?" I said. "What's going on?"

"I gotta go," Frank said, crying harder now. "The cops are gonna take me to ID the body."

"Where?"

"Brooklyn."

"*What?*"

"Lemme outta here."

"This is crazy," I said. "There's gotta be some mistake."

"It's not a mistake!"

"How do you know?"

"She didn't come home last night. She—just lemme get the hell out of here."

Frank left the bar. Through the window, I watched him get into the police car with the two cops and drive away.

I knew I'd played it good. Frank was such a mess now, he couldn't think straight about anything. Later on, when he started to calm down, he still wouldn't suspect me. He'd think some guy she met in one of those personal ads killed her. And if he *did* suspect me, he'd remember how I'd acted when he was leaving the bar to go ID the body. He'd remember how I was just as surprised as he was, saying all the things that inno-cent people usually say.

When I went back to the bar, I told Gil what was going on. He didn't believe me at first—I had to tell him three or four times. Then, his eyes starting to tear, he said, "Man, I can't believe this. The poor guy. Jesus."

"It's so fucked up," I said sadly, shaking my head.

Gil asked me if I thought we should shut down the bar tonight.

"I don't think so," I said. "Frank didn't tell me we should do that and, besides, maybe that wasn't Debbie's body they found out there. Maybe she'll walk right in here any second."

I went into the kitchen. Rodrigo was there, talking in Spanish to the Mexican dishwasher. They shut up when they saw me.

"Excuse me, can I talk to Rodrigo alone for a second?" I said to the dishwasher.

The kid gave me a dumb look, like he didn't under-stand English. Rodrigo translated then the kid left.

"What do you want for me?" Rodrigo said.

"*From* me," I said.

Rodrigo started to leave.

"Hold up a second, all right?" I said. "I wanna have this out."

Rodrigo stopped, waiting for me to go on.

"We both work here, right?" I said. "So what's the point of going around, acting like we hate each other? I don't know about you, but I think it's a big pain in the ass. The way I look at it, we both made mistakes, so why not just clear the air and forget about it? I don't know about you, but I'm not holding a grudge—I have no hard feelings. So what do you say, Rodrigo? Are we *amigos*?"

For a few seconds, Rodrigo just stood there, not saying a word. Then he said something in Spanish and walked out of the kitchen.

I was worried about Rodrigo. I didn't think he'd rat on me and risk being deported, but I'd have to keep an eye on him just in case.

I cooked myself a couple of thick burgers, then I went back out front. It was starting to get busy again so I went up to the bar to give Gil a hand. Gil had obviously broken the news to Kathy. She was in bad shape, crying, and I told her not to worry—everything would be all right.

I knew that the police would be by the bar at some point tonight, probably after Frank ID'd Debbie's body, but I wasn't worried about it. It was bad luck that they'd found her so fast—at first, I had to admit, it scared the shit out of me—but now I knew it didn't really mean anything. The police still wouldn't have any idea who'd killed her because there was no evidence. Just to be safe, later tonight I'd clean the rest of the mud out of my car, and then I'd just keep on doing what I was doing and everything would work out fine.

I wasn't even worried when the *Eyewitness News* truck pulled up in front of the bar and a female reporter I recognized from TV came inside with a guy holding a camera. Everybody was watching when the woman came up to me at the bar.

"I'm Marcia Cole from *Eyewitness News*. Do you work here?"

"Yeah," I said.

"Did you know Deborah O'Reilley?"

"Sure I knew her."

"Would you like to make a comment for our cameras?"

"All right," I said. "Why not?"

Gil lowered the music and asked everybody in the bar to quiet down. The cameraman shined a bright light on me and said, "Rolling." Then, sticking a big mike in my face, Marcia said, "Did you know Deborah O'Reilley well?"

"Not too well," I said. "But we talked whenever she came into the bar."

"Were you surprised to hear that something like this happened to her?"

"Very. I just can't believe it—I just can't. She always seemed so happy, like she didn't have an enemy in the world. This is really a shock. It's just a shock, that's all I can say."

"Do you think this murder has anything to do with the robbery of the Super Bowl money from the safe the other day?"

"I don't know," I said. "I don't see how it would."

"Do you think Deborah O'Reilley's stepson, Gary O'Reilley, had anything to do with the murder or the robbery?"

"I don't know," I said. "I hope not."

"Thank you," Marcia said and the cameraman stopped shooting. Then Maria said to Gil, "Would you like to say something for the cameras too?"

Gil made a brief statement then Marcia started talking to other people in the bar. A few minutes later, the other news crews started to arrive. Channel Four was there first, then Channel Five, Channel Eleven, and New York 1, and then the radio and newspaper people showed up. It was getting out of control and Gil came over and asked me if I thought we should shut down the bar. I told him I thought this was probably a good idea.

I turned off the music and told everybody they had to leave their drinks and go home. There was a lot of bitching and moaning but after a few minutes everybody was gone except the reporters. The new reporters wanted me to say something for the cameras so I said pretty much the same thing I'd said for *Eyewitness News*. I liked having all those cameras and lights pointed at me. I felt like I was acting again. I was in a movie or on a TV show and I knew this was only the beginning. When I was a famous horse owner I'd be holding news conferences all the time.

Then, when I was finishing up the interview, looking past the cameras and mikes, with the bright light in my eyes, I saw Cheryl Lewis, the blond cop who'd been in the bar the other day. She was with another cop and the same detective who'd asked me questions. I stared at her until she saw me and then we both smiled.

"Hey," I said when she came up to the bar. "Long time no see."

"I wish I was here under more pleasant circumstances."

"Fuckin' sucks, doesn't it?" I said. "I still can't believe it. Do they know what happened to her yet?"

"Suffocation was the probable cause of death, but they're still running tests."

"Jesus," I said, shaking my head.

"Did you know her very well?"

"Not too well," I said. "I mean just from the bar. So are you working on this case too?"

"No, investigators from Homicide will be handling it. We're just here for routine reasons. Since the robbery was only a few days ago, we want to see if that had anything to do with this."

"The robbery—I didn't even think about that," I said. "You think the robbery has something to do with my boss's wife—"

"You never know," she said. "In any case, we might be able to provide the Homicide detectives with any details they might need."

"Anybody ever tell you you have beautiful eyes?"

She looked uncomfortable.

"I'm engaged," she said.

I looked down at her left hand and sure enough she was wearing a big rock—probably cost the guy ten grand. It was so big and shiny, I didn't know how I could've missed it the other day.

"So?" I said. "I'm just complimenting you. What, you're gonna arrest me for that?"

She smiled.

"Sorry," she said. "I'm just working overtime today and it's been a very long day. Thank you very much—for your compliment, I mean."

"No problem," I said. "So what do you do when you're not trying to catch crooks?"

"Excuse me?"

"You like movies, dancing, Italian food…"

"Why are you doing this?"

"Doing what?"

"Didn't you understand what I told you? I'm engaged."

"That doesn't mean we can't go out sometime, does it? I mean I don't want you to do anything you don't want to do, but I'd love to take you out to dinner on my next night off."

"I'm sorry," she said.

"That's okay," I said. "Maybe some other time."

A few minutes later, a couple of other detectives arrived and asked all the reporters to leave the bar. One of the detectives looked familiar, but I didn't know why. He was a big guy—about my height, but

fatter—and he had short blond hair. He saw me noticing him and came over to the bar.

"You mind if I ask you a couple of questions?" he
said to me. He had a Brooklyn accent.

"No problem," I said.

He took out a little notepad.

"My name is Detective Scott. I work in Homicide—
Brooklyn South. And you are?"

Hearing that name, Scott, made it all click.

"Mikey?" I said.

The detective looked up from the pad.

"Do I know you?"

"It's me—Tommy. Tommy Russo. Remember—
Sophomore year, the Canarsie High football team. I
played left tackle, you were center."

The detective was still staring at me. For a second,
I thought I'd made a mistake, but then he smiled and
said, "Holy shit, Tommy fuckin' Russo. How the hell
are you?"

We shook hands.

"I can't believe you didn't recognize me," I said.
"What, I look so much different?"

"Well, you look like you might've put on a few LBs."

"Look who's talking," I said.

We laughed.

"So what've you been doing for, what, the past fifteen
years?"

"I work here," I said.

"I see that. What are you, a bartender?"

"Bouncer," I said.

"Tough guy."

"Yeah, you know how it is. What about you? How long you been a cop?"

"I've been with the department eleven years, a detective for three."

"I always knew you were gonna go places."

"I'd love to catch up, but we better just get down to business here," Mike said. "This is all routine, but I just gotta ask you a few questions here."

"Shoot," I said.

He asked me some questions—how long have I been working at the bar, did I know Debbie O'Reilley, and other questions I could've answered without even thinking. Then he said, "And can you tell me what your whereabouts were last night?"

He must've seen the look I was giving him because then he said, "This is all routine. We just try to get little snapshots of the way things were last night and it helps us put a bigger picture together."

"I was working at the bar," I said.

"When did you arrive?"

"Around six."

"And when did you leave?"

"Early—around eleven-thirty. I was fuckin' zonked. I got home from Vegas three o'clock yesterday afternoon."

"What were you doing in Vegas?"

"Losing my balls, getting laid. The usual."

Mike smiled, writing in his notepad.

"Let me ask you something else," Mike said. "Do you think Gary O'Reilley would kill his stepmother?"

"That's what the reporters were asking me before. Jesus, I don't know. I mean I know the kid was hot-headed, but I hope he didn't do something like that."

"What do you mean, 'hot-headed'?"

"I don't wanna bad-mouth the guy, but let's just say he had a problem with the way Debbie treated Frank."

"For example…"

"He'd say things to me about how much he hated her. I mean, I don't know if you heard, but Debbie was a real slut. She'd come in here all the time with guys, shooting her mouth off in front of Frank, and Gary wouldn't do anything, but you could tell it was pissing him off. Then he'd say things to me, about how he wanted to kill her, get rid of her, shit like that."

"He said he wanted to kill her?"

"Yeah, I guess he did. I'm not saying I think he meant it. I mean a lot of people say shit like that when they're mad. But he did say it—a couple of times."

"How many times?"

"Jesus, I don't know. Two or three. Maybe it was more than that."

"Did he tell you anything specific? I mean did he say he had a weapon of any kind?"

"No, nothing like that. Like I said, it was just talk."

"Did you see Gary O'Reilley yesterday?"

"Nah, I haven't seen him since Monday night, when he stormed out of here."

"Why'd he do that?"

"He had a fight with Frank. Frank wanted to make me manager of the bar when he moved to Arizona and Gary was pretty pissed off."

"Detective Edwards here tells me that you were the one who saw Gary outside the bar the night the safe was robbed."

"That's right," I said.

"What about Frank O'Reilley?"

"What about him?"

"You think he could've killed his wife?"

"Frank? No way."

"How could you be so sure?"

"First of all, whoever killed Debbie was an animal and Frank doesn't have a sick bone in his body. Second of all, the guy loved his wife."

"You said Debbie O'Reilley was always showing him up to his face. Maybe it got to him and he snapped."

"I guess it's possible," I said. "I mean you know what they say—you never know people. But I'd really be surprised."

Mike finished writing in his notepad.

"Well, that about takes care of it for now. You know, you better give me your phone number and address because I got a feeling we're gonna need some more info from you."

I gave him my info then I said, "So you got any hot leads?"

"We have your boss down at the precinct in Brooklyn right now and some colleagues of mine are talking to him. Most likely, one of her lover boys rubbed her out. The wrong guy answered one of her ads and she got whacked—it happens all the time."

"Sick fucks."

"You got that right."

Mike went back across the bar to talk to the other detective. The two cops who came in before—including Cheryl—were gone. They must've taken off while I was talking to Mike.

The next hour or two were pretty boring. Mike and the other detectives were sitting at a table talking and Gil was sitting at the bar, reading some book. Kathy hung out awhile, then she went home. Rodrigo and the other guys from the kitchen took off too. I wanted to leave, but I knew that wouldn't look good. It would be better to stick around—make it look like I had nothing to hide. Mike said that Frank was going to be escorted back to the bar, after he was through at the precinct in Brooklyn, and that's another reason I wanted to stay. Frank seemed like he was in pretty bad shape before and I wanted to be around when he came back, just in case there was anything I could do to help him.

I brought over a round of Cokes for the detectives, then I turned on the TV and watched hockey highlights on ESPN. I watched a basketball game on TNT—the Suns and the Sixers—even though I hated pro basketball and I didn't care who won.

Frank walked into the bar at around eleven o'clock. His eyes were red and swollen and his thin gray hair was a mess. He sat down with the detectives for a while, answering more questions. He wasn't crying anymore but he looked out of it. After about a half hour, the detectives got up to leave. Mike came over to the bar and shook my hand. He said he might be in touch, if not he hoped we ran into each other again sometime. Then he leaned over the bar and whispered in my ear, "You might want to make sure your boss gets home all right tonight, buddy."

When the detectives were gone I went over to the table and sat down across from Frank. "You want me to put you in a cab?"

"It's all right," he said. "I could use a nice stiff one though."

I made Frank a gin and tonic, doubling up on the gin. I told Gil that it would probably be a good idea if he took off. He went to the back to get his jacket. On his way out, he shook Frank's hand and said, "I just want you to know, I'm here for you if you need me."

Gil left and it was just me and Frank alone in the bar. I sat across from him, watching him sip his drink. It was quiet and I wasn't going to say anything until Frank did. I knew how he had always treated me like a son, and I knew that as his son the right thing to do was to just sit there and not say a word.

Finally Frank said, like we were in the middle of a conversation, "They say I might need a lawyer."

"A lawyer?" I said. "Why?"

"Why do you think? You know what they were doing back there in Brooklyn? They were grilling me like I'm a goddamn criminal. They showed me the body—it was her all right—and I almost passed out. Then they take me into a room and I think they're gonna give me counseling or something, treat me for trauma. But you know what those sons of bitches do instead? They start laying it into me, asking me where I was last night, when was the last time I saw Debbie alive. I probably should've shut up and demanded a lawyer, but I was in shock. I mean those guys really think I killed my wife "

"I wouldn't knock myself out about it if I were you," I said. Those questions were probably just routine. Before you got here, the cops were talking to me, Gil, Kathy and the guys from the kitchen too. I wouldn't take it personal…"

"They want my blood."

"You mean they wanna get you or they really want your blood?"

"Both. The Medical Examiner or the coroner—or whatever the hell they're called—they found some forensic evidence on Debbie's body and they want to try to match the DNA."

"No kidding?" I said, trying to stay calm.

"Can you believe that? These fucking detectives think I'm some wacko—that I'd kill my wife and then dump her in Brooklyn. I told the cops—I don't know my ass from my elbow about Brooklyn. If I was gonna kill my wife why would I dump her there? It's just fuckin' crazy—crazy."

"You should really get home and get some rest," I said. Want me to put you in a cab now?"

"In a minute," Frank said. "Lemme finish this drink first." He took another sip then said, "You know what kills me—Fred Fucking Harrison, that detective I hired. If he just did his job, if he was following Debbie last night like he was supposed to—"

"Hey, you can't look at things that way," I said. "I mean things happen and then they're over and you just gotta forget about them."

"I know what you're saying," Frank said, "but still. I just wish there was something I could've done. I mean I tried to do everything, but she just wouldn't listen to me. It's not my fault. I didn't want this to happen."

Frank covered his face and started to cry.

Finally, after a couple of minutes, he got himself together. He finished the rest of his drink in one gulp, then said, "I gotta get the hell outta here. Do me a favor? Close up for me tonight, will ya?"

"No problem, buddy. Want me to get you that cab?"

"No, it's all right. Hey, Tommy, before I go, I want to ask you one question and I want a straight answer. No bullshit, all right? I want the truth. Just look me in the eye and say it—don't hold back."

Jesus, not again. Just like the other night when he wanted me to tell him that I didn't rob the safe, now he wanted me to tell him that I didn't kill his wife. I was ready to get angry again, like anybody would when somebody accuses them of doing something they didn't do, but then Frank said, "Do you think I did it, Tommy? You think I killed her?"

I stood there for a second then I hugged him tightly and slapped him on the back a couple of times.

"Of course I don't think that," I said. "I can't believe you just asked me that question."

"Thanks, Tommy. That means a lot to me."

I walked him out to the sidewalk and watched him get into a cab.

Back in the bar, I chugged a pint of Sam Adams, wondering about this forensic evidence. Although I'd started to have sex with Debbie that night, I didn't finish, so I knew they didn't have my semen. I didn't bleed on her either, so they couldn't have my blood. The evidence had probably come from someone else, or maybe there wasn't any evidence at all—the police had made a mistake. I didn't think I had anything to worry about.

I had another beer, then I stacked all the chairs and bar stools. When the front of the bar was all set, I went back to the kitchen and made sure everything was off and put away. Then I put my coat on and went into the bathroom and put about a dozen moistened paper towels into my coat pocket. I shut all the lights, set the alarm, and went outside and pulled down the gates and bolted the locks.

It wasn't as cold as it had been the past couple of nights. All the snow was gone from the sidewalks and there was no wind. I felt so good I opened the top couple of buttons on my coat and felt the nice cool breeze against my chest.

I turned onto my block, but instead of going into my apartment I went to my car. I looked around to make sure nobody was watching me, then I opened the door. With the paper towels I scrubbed the dry mud off the seat, the floor, the dashboard and the steering wheel. It came off a lot easier than I'd thought and after a couple of minutes it was all gone. Leaning across the scat, I was about to stand up when I heard somebody behind me. My stomach sank as I wondered if it could be a cop standing there. I stood up and turned around and let out a deep breath. It was just a homeless guy passing by, mumbling to himself.

I went up to my apartment and got naked. Then I shut the light and got into bed. I turned onto my side thinking about the outfit I'd wear for my first day as a horse owner.

Fifteen

On the morning news, there was footage from Marine Park, Brooklyn. Ambulance workers were carrying Debbie's body away on a stretcher, covered by a white sheet. Then there was a shot of O'Reilley's and the reporter was talking about how Debbie O'Reilley was the wife of the guy who owned the bar and how the Super Bowl pool was robbed last Saturday night. The reporter said that the police were searching for Frank O'Reilley's son, Gary O'Reilley, who was suspected of robbing the safe. "According to a police spokesperson," the reporter said, "Gary O'Reilley is not necessarily a suspect in the case—police would just like to question him." Then a detective I never saw before came on and said, "At this point we can't rule out any possibilities. Right now all we'd like to do is find Gary O'Reilley and see if he can assist us in any way. But since he is missing at this time, and since a homicide in his family has taken place, there may also be reason to fear for his safety." Then I came on. I was behind the bar, saying how shocked I was and how I never thought something like this could happen. But it didn't really matter what I was saying because I wasn't hearing the words. I was in a daze, staring at myself, thinking about how natural I looked on TV. My beard was coming in nice and thick and I looked relaxed and confident. Some people on TV looked like they didn't belong there, but not me. I looked like a movie star.

The story ended. I got up and stared at myself in the bathroom mirror, first thinking about how great I looked, then thinking about how the cops weren't going to catch me.

I moved my car to a legal spot around the corner, then I went to the supermarket. I only had about fifty dollars to my name, but I wanted to eat some food for a change. I bought cheeses—Swiss, cheddar, and a pack of those little triangle cheeses that come in the foil wrappers. I also bought a couple of kinds of dips and boxes of crackers. My days of hot dogs, pizza and sleazy diners were over with—from now on I was going to do everything in class.

When I came home the phone was ringing.

"Tommy, it's Costas."

My fucking landlord.

"What's up?" I said, still catching my breath from the walk up the stairs.

"Maybe you should tell me that," he said. "How come you don't return my calls? I've been calling you every day for a week."

"I've been busy lately."

"Busy? What about my building? I get calls from tenants—the building is a mess, it's not being cleaned.

Everybody has mice, roaches. Garbage is piled in the halls. So then I came by yesterday and I see for myself. I couldn't believe it! You don't think I'm letting you pay that cheap rent for doing nothing, do you?"

"I've *been* cleaning," I said.

"Cleaning? Your cleaning is shit. You think I'm paying you for nothing? You think I'm giving you charity? You think—"

I hung up on him. A few seconds later, the phone was ringing again.

"What is it?" I said, ready to pull the cord out of the wall.

"Yes, I'm trying to get in touch with Tommy Russo." It was a man's voice.

"Who's this?"

"Detective Scott...it's Mike, Tommy."

"Hey, Mikey, I thought it was...never mind. How's it going?"

"Pretty good. I was wondering if you had some time today, if we could ask you a few more questions."

"What's up?"

"Not much," he said. "We just have some more developments. This shouldn't take too long and it'd really help us out."

"What's it about?"

"Just routine—we're talking to everybody from the bar."

"I'm kinda busy," I said. "I gotta be at work by five."

"It shouldn't take too long—an hour tops. We're over at the 19th Precinct on Sixty-seventh Street be-

tween Third and Lex. I'd appreciate it if you came by
here around two o'clock."

"All right, I'll be by."

"Thanks, buddy."

I showed up at the precinct at two o'clock on the
button. Mike came up front to meet me. He looked
the same as he did last night—wearing what looked
like the same shirt and tie. We shook hands and then
he led me to a room in the back. There were three
guys sitting on one side of the long table—the only one
I recognized was the detective who was investigating
the robbery. Mike sat down next to them and told me
to sit down in the one seat on the other side of the
table. It didn't look like this was going to be "routine."

One of the guys said, "I'm Detective Himoto, Mr.
Russo. Thank you for coming down here today."

Himoto was Japanese-American, but he spoke
English without an accent.

"No problem," I said.

"This is Detective Howard," Himoto said, and the
black guy next to him nodded, "and I think you've already met Detective Edwards. We just wanted to run
through a few things with you, Mr. Russo, if that's all
right with you?"

"I'll do whatever I can to help," I said.

"First of all," Himoto said, "we'd like you to take a
look at this."

He slid a sheet of paper across the desk to me. I
picked it up and read to myself.

Mama, mama can't breathe no more
Mama, mama always there, ain't no cure
Mama, mama you better run
'Cause it sure as hell ain't gonna be no fun

"Yeah," I said, sliding the paper back across the table. "So?"

"These are lyrics to a song we found in Gary O'Reilley's apartment last night."

"Well it doesn't sound like he's gonna be the next Michael Jackson, huh?" I said smiling.

All the detectives smiled with me, except Himoto.

"The lyrics to several of his other songs also had homicidal themes," Himoto said. "Did Gary ever talk to you about his homicidal fantasies, particularly ones involving his stepmother?"

"No, I told Mike—I mean Detective Scott—last night that I couldn't imagine the guy killing anybody."

"Sorry to be redundant, Mr. Russo, but we have to be as thorough as possible with our investigation. That's how a police investigation works. At this point, we don't know what's important and what isn't, so we just have to assume everything is important and work from there. So I'd appreciate your cooperation and patience."

I didn't like the way Himoto was talking down to me in front of the other detectives.

"No problem," I said. "Like I said, I just wanna help you guys any way I can."

"Has Gary O'Reilley tried to contact you?" Himoto asked.

"You kidding? He hardly speaks to me."

"Why's that?"

"It's just one of those things. I guess we don't have a lot in common."

"Do you know any friends of his he could be staying with?"

I shook my head.

"No friends of his ever came to the bar?"

"Yeah, once in a while, but I didn't know any of them. I mean maybe if you showed me some pictures I could pick somebody out. Except, come to think of it, there was a guy from his band who came to the bar to meet him sometimes. He had a ponytail, but I don't know his name."

"We've talked to his band members," Himoto said. "I was hoping you knew of somebody else. Maybe somebody who lives in Brooklyn."

"Sorry," I said.

"What about Gary O'Reilley's relationship with his stepmother?"

"What about it?"

"Would you describe them as close?"

"No, not really. I mean the way Debbie drank it was hard for anyone to get close with her."

"Is it possible that they were closer than they seemed?" Himoto asked.

"What do you mean?"

"A witness we spoke with said that he thought he once saw Gary and Debbie holding hands. Do you think it's possible that they…something funny Mr. Russo?"

"Sorry," I said, realizing I must've been smiling. "It's just the idea of Gary and Debbie together like that is kind of sick. It's impossible too."

"Why is it impossible? We understand that Debbie was quite promiscuous."

"That's true, she was," I said. "But let's just say that I don't think women are exactly Gary's type."

"Did you know that Gary O'Reilley has a girlfriend?"

"No, I didn't know that."

"Well, he does. Let me ask you something else, Mr. Russo. Do you have something against homosexuals?"

"What do you mean?"

"You just seem to have a sarcastic-aggressive attitude about the subject. My son happens to be gay so I'd appreciate it if you put your personal feelings aside during the rest of this conversation. Do you think you can do that?"

"No problem," I said, wondering why Himoto seemed to have it in for me.

Himoto let out a deep breath then said, "Detective Scott tells me you saw Gary at the bar on Monday night. Do you remember what time he left?"

"Jesus, lemme think," I said. "It must've been a little after six o'clock."

"And what did you do after that?"

"I stayed till closing time, then I caught some shut-eye. Tuesday morning I went to Vegas."

"Was this a planned trip?"

"No, not really," I said. "But I had a couple of days to kill so I figured I'd go away."

Himoto looked at the other detectives, then he stood up and said, "I think that's all we need from you for right now, Mr. Russo. Thanks for coming down."

"I want you guys to know something," I said.

Himoto turned back toward me. The other detectives were looking at me too.

"Gary O'Reilley hates my guts," I said. "He thinks his father likes me better than him, which he probably does, and he's pissed that Frank wants to let me manage the bar when he moves to Arizona. When you find him he's gonna say all kinds of shit about me. I just wanted you guys to know that."

"Thanks again for your time, Mr. Russo," Himoto said, and he left the room.

The other detectives walked out too, except Mike.

"So what's the deal with Himoto?" I asked.

"Don't worry about him," Mike said. "You just hit a sore spot with him, that's all. His kid's a major-league homo, an AIDS activist, the whole nine yards."

"So they really think Gary did it, huh?" I said.

"Maybe," Mike said. "They have some DNA evidence they're gonna run by the lab—see if it brings a match."

"What kind of evidence?" I asked.

"They found a couple of pubes on the body," Mike said. "Some guy was probably balling her before she died."

Mike walked me to the front of the precinct, updating me about the rest of the case. He said that the cops still didn't know much about Debbie's where-

abouts before she was killed. She was last seen at a
Chinese restaurant on Second Avenue at around 4:30
Wednesday afternoon, but they had no idea where she
went after that or how her body wound up in Brooklyn.
At the door, Mike thanked me again for coming down
and he said he doubted he'd need to talk to me again.
We shook hands goodbye.

Sixteen

Things at work seemed to be going back to normal. There were no cops or reporters around—just the usual cronies, finishing up getting drunk before they went home to their wives. Kathy had the night off, but Gil was sitting on a stool, writing in his little notebook, and even Frank was there, sitting at a table alone, nursing a beer. It kind of surprised me to see Frank at the bar, after the way he was last night, but it made a lot of sense too. Maybe he finally realized that Debbie was just a big headache and he was a lot better off with her out of the way.

"Hey," I said, sitting down across from him.

"Hey, Tommy," he said, looking up. He seemed happy to see me.

"You look a lot better than you did last night," I said.

"I look like shit and you know it," he said. "I wouldn't have come in, but I didn't know what else to do with myself. I was up all night on the phone with Debbie's relatives. Now I've got a funeral to plan."

"Hey, if you want me to take care of that I can," I said.

"I appreciate it, Tommy, but that's all right. My sister's coming up from Maryland and she'll help out. It's just hard, you know?"

"You just gotta hang in there—be strong," I said. "I was by the police precinct before."

"Yeah, they had Gil and Gary there too."

"Gary? I thought they—"

"That's the good news. The police said Gary isn't a suspect anymore."

"Why not?"

"He had an alibi for Wednesday, the time they think Debbie was killed. He was at his friend's house in Astoria."

"That *is* good news," I said. "Lemme go hang up my coat."

It turned out to be the slowest Friday night I'd ever seen at O'Reilley's. By eight o'clock there were only two customers in the bar, then they left and the place was empty.

I was back by the bar, playing a Queen CD, when Rodrigo walked in. He glared at me with dark, pissed-off eyes, then he sat down at the table across from Frank. Over "We Will Rock You" I couldn't make out what Rodrigo was saying, but I didn't like the looks of it. A few times, Frank looked over at me, and I knew Rodrigo was telling Frank about the robbery. I couldn't understand why he was telling him now, after he'd kept the secret for so long.

Rodrigo sat at the table with Frank for a while longer—Rodrigo doing all the talking, Frank just sitting there, looking over at me once in a while, taking it in. Then Rodrigo got up and, without looking at me, went toward the kitchen. I was going to follow him, find out what the hell was going on, when Frank got up and came over to me, sitting down on a stool across the bar.

"Let me guess," I said before Frank could say anything. "Rodrigo was trying to get me back."

"Get you back?" Frank asked.

"We had a little incident here the other night when you weren't around," I said, smiling. "His wife came into the bar and I didn't know she was his wife—I just thought she was a good-looking Mexican girl. And you know how I am when I see a pretty face. I started talking to her, just polite talk, and Rodrigo saw us and flipped out. You know, Mexicans with their *machismo*. The fuckin' guy thought I was trying to pick up his wife." I laughed. "Anyway, he got all hot-headed, started calling me names and I said something about his mother. I guess now he's getting me back by telling you shit about me. Am I right?"

"He said you robbed the safe."

"I knew it. You'd think the guy could've come up with a more original way to get even than to start making up rumors about me. What does he think this is, high school?"

Frank was staring at me.

"What?" I said. "Don't tell me you believe that bullshit?"

"You went to Vegas Monday night?"

"Yeah," I said, figuring the cops must've told him so there was no point denying it. "So what?"

"I was gonna say something about it before, but now

it all makes sense. Where the hell did you get the money to go to Las Vegas?"

Frank was screaming. I'd never heard him scream before, at anybody, but I decided not to take it personally. He was probably just pissed off about all the shit that was happening lately and he was taking it out on me.

"I hit at the track," I said calmly.

"I thought you told me you weren't gonna bet anymore?"

"What can I say?" I said. "I've got a problem. And if you wanna know the truth I've signed up for Gamblers Anonymous."

"Rodrigo told me he saw you leave here that night, carrying a big garbage bag."

"Rodrigo's a liar."

"I've been through too much the past twenty-four hours to put up with any more bullshit," he said. "To be honest, I don't really care about the robbery anymore, but I just want to know the truth now, once and for all—"

"I told you the truth. Come on, I don't even know the combination to the safe, remember?"

"Maybe you saw me or Gary going into it one time."

"That's crazy. Don't listen to Rodrigo. If Rodrigo saw me steal the money why wouldn't he've told you right away?"

Frank took a deep breath. "He said he would've told me about it right away, but he was afraid to get involved with the police because he was working here illegally."

"So why is he telling you now?"

"His green card just came through this afternoon."

"Come on," I said. "The guy's lying—he probably took that money himself and now he's just trying to cover his own ass."

While I was talking, Gary stormed into the bar. He looked crazy. His hair was a mess and he looked tired, like he hadn't slept since the last time I saw him. Swinging his arms, he walked around the bar and came right up to me.

"He did it," Gary said to Frank. "I told you right away, but you didn't believe me. First he robbed you, then he killed Debbie."

"Hey, watch your fuckin' mouth," I said.

Now Gil came over and he was standing behind Gary.

"Why don't you just cool it?" Gil said.

"Stay the hell out of this," Gary said. "This is between me and this killer right here."

"Hey," I said to Frank, "if you don't tell your kid to shut up—"

"She was flirting with him all the time," Gary said to Frank. "If you didn't know about it you were blind, because everybody knew about it."

"Look," I said. "If you don't just shut the hell—"

Gary sucker-punched me below my left eye and I stumbled backwards into the liquor bottles. Glass crashed onto the floor. Frank and Gil were screaming and Queen was singing "We Are The Champions." I was okay, though. I didn't fall down and I wasn't dazed. My eye hurt and I knew it was going to swell up if

I didn't put ice on it. But the ice would have to wait.

"That was for Debbie," Gary said, "and for my father."

Frank was yelling at us and Gil was trying to hold Gary back. Then Gary got loose. He took another swing at me, but this time I was ready. I stepped back and the punch missed wildly. I saw my opening. I pushed him off me then I hit him with an uppercut to the jaw. His head snapped back first, then his whole body went. As he was falling backwards, I caught him again—right in the mouth. It was probably the hardest I'd ever hit anybody. I got all my strength behind it and he didn't have a chance to duck. He fell straight back on his ass like somebody pulled a rug out from under him.

"That's all," Frank said. He was grabbing me from behind. "Get the hell out of here—right now!"

Gary was squirming around on the ground, trying to get up. Blood was dripping from his mouth. Then he spit a few teeth onto the floor.

"Look what you did," he mumbled. "Look what you did." He was crying.

"Gil, pick up the teeth and put them on ice," Frank said. "Maybe a dentist can reattach them."

Gil took a glass and started to put the bloody teeth into it.

Frank was looking at me.

"I had to do it," I said. "You saw him take that cheap shot at me."

"I want you out of here! Now!"

"Frank, come on, I—"

"Out!"

Gil helped Gary up. Gary looked like he was about to pass out.

"Take him to the bathroom in the back and clean him up," Frank said. "Then we'll take him to a dentist."

Frank took the glass with the teeth and put ice in it. After Gary and Gil passed by I started to leave. Then I turned back toward Frank.

"Before I go I just want you to know I'm not lying," I said. "I don't know who robbed the safe or who killed your wife, but it sure as hell wasn't me. You know that."

Frank didn't say anything.

I waited a few seconds then said, "And don't worry about those choppers. An old buddy of mine got his teeth busted once. The dentist put on some of those caps and the guy came back looking like a movie star."

"You better just go home, Tommy."

"All right," I said. "Whatever you say. I mean you're the boss, right?"

I went to the back to get my leather coat. When I came back, Frank was sitting on a bar stool with his head in his hands. I couldn't tell if he was crying, but he was moving his head like he was. I really felt sorry for him.

"I still want to manage this bar some day," I said. "I know I can do a great job for you and if you want me to do it I'll do it. But if you don't want me back here, that's fine with me too. I just want you to know, you're still like a father to me."

I started to leave.

"Tommy."

I turned around. Suddenly, Frank looked ten years older.

"See you tomorrow," he said.

I smiled, then I flipped up my coat collar and I left the bar.

Seventeen

At seven A.M. I was standing in front of the mirror on
my closet door. I was wearing my white suit with my
black shirt, shiny black shoes, a black tie, and my lucky
gold barbell chain. My hair was slicked back and my
beard was trimmed. I would've looked perfect if it
weren't for my black eye. I hadn't put ice on it and it
had swelled up overnight.

The gates to the racetrack didn't open until eleven
o'clock, but I wanted to leave early. Sunshine Brandy
was running in the second race and I was afraid that if
something happened, like my car broke down, I'd miss
it. But leaving six hours before the race went off I'd
definitely get there with time to spare.

On my way out, I checked the kitchen counter. Last
night, when I came home from the bar, I'd noticed
more cheese was gone and there were some more
droppings. Now there were only two chunks of cheese
left and the whole counter was covered with mouse
shit. I took the rest of the cheese out of the fridge,
spread it around the counter for the mice to feast on,
and then I got the show on the road.

My car started right away and it made it on to the
FDR Drive without stalling. One of the first things I
was going to do when I got rich was buy a new car—

probably a bright red Ferrari. Or maybe I'd have a few cars, just to mix things up.

There was no traffic so I made it to the track in about an hour. I thought about going to a diner to kill time and grab something to eat, but I didn't have an appetite. I was too excited to eat and, besides, I remembered how I'd promised myself that my diner days were over. I'd only go to expensive restaurants to eat from now on, but I didn't figure there were too many nice restaurants in Ozone Park, Queens, near the racetrack—especially not ones that were open at eight in the morning.

You might think that time would go by slowly, sitting in a parked car with nothing to do, but the next time I checked my watch it was eleven o'clock.

I pulled into the parking lot, paying the extra buck for preferred parking, and then I sat there for a minute, letting it all soak in. I realized how much my life had improved in the past two weeks. That day at the jai-alai fronton I was a struggling actor with no prospects, but now everything was working out. No doubt about it—Pete Logan getting into my car was probably the best thing that had ever happened to me.

Walking slowly so I wouldn't sweat up my suit, I headed toward the entrance to the clubhouse. The old guy at the admission window didn't even look at me as he took my three bucks. When I was a famous horse owner I knew things would be a lot different. I'd probably have a pass, go through a special entrance, and the guy at the door would say "Good morning, Mr. Russo," and if he was lucky I'd look at him or say good morning back.

Going into the track, I felt like I was stepping into my new life. Outside was the old Tommy Russo, and I wasn't sad to see him go.

I went to the bathroom to piss and to make sure I still looked great. A few hairs had come loose, but I slicked them back into place with some water and my little black comb, and then I went back into the clubhouse. I decided to go out to the stands and take a look at the owners' boxes—see where I'd be sitting someday. But on my way out a tall, skinny black usher, said, "You got a pass?"

"No. I mean not yet," I said.

"Then you can't go out there."

"It's all right. I just wanted to look."

"Sorry. You can't go out there if you don't got a pass."

"But I just wanted to take a look, that's all."

I started to walk by him. He stood in my way.

"Those are the owners' boxes," he said. "They're only for authorized personnel."

"I'm gonna be authorized personnel. I'm claiming a horse today."

"Sorry," he said, "if you're not authorized personnel you can't go out there."

"I just wanna go take a look," I said. "What's the big deal?"

I walked past him and he grabbed the back of my shoulder.

"Hey," I said. "What's your problem?"

Or maybe I yelled it because a security guard came running over.

"What's going on here?" he asked. He was a little old Irish guy with gray hair and square shoulders. He reminded me of Frank.

"Ask this guy," I said. "He just grabbed me."

"I just told him he can't go out there without a pass and he tried to get by me," the usher said.

"Forget about it," I said. "The guy's crazy."

"Just take it easy," the security guard said. "I don't want any trouble here."

"You talking to me or him?" I said.

"You," he said.

I walked away, shaking my head.

I spotted Pete, sitting on a bench against the wall, reading the *Racing Form*. At first I thought it couldn't possibly be him. Not because he looked different, because he looked the *same*. He was wearing sneakers, old jeans, a hooded sweatshirt, and the same beige winter jacket he'd been wearing at the jai-alai fronton. He wasn't even dressed up as good as he was at the Chinese restaurant. Maybe I got the day screwed up— maybe we were supposed to claim the horse tomorrow or some other time. I couldn't think of any other reason why Pete wasn't wearing a suit.

When I walked over to him he looked up at me like he was surprised. I was probably giving him the same look.

"Look at you," he said, "all decked out. What's the special occasion?"

Maybe I *did* get the date mixed up.

"What do you mean?" I said. "I got a call from Alan the other day. We're claiming the horse today, right?"

"If he doesn't get scratched," Pete said. "But I just checked the board downstairs and he's still in. No, I meant are you doing something after the races? Going to a wedding or something?"

"No," I said.

"Then what's with the outfit?"

"I was gonna ask you the same question," I said.

"What do you mean? I always dress like this to go to the track."

"That's what I mean," I said.

We stared at each other for a couple of seconds.

"I get it," Pete said. "You're trying to be funny."

"Do I look like I'm trying to be funny?" I said. "I don't understand—why did you dress like that today?"

"Because I felt like it," he said.

"Yeah, well you're a horse owner now—you should dress like one. Is this how you're gonna look when you're down there in the winner's circle, getting your picture taken? I mean come on—"

"Are you feeling all right?" Pete asked.

"Are *you*?"

"Maybe you should sit down—relax."

I turned around and started to walk away. Then I stopped, realizing this wouldn't do me any good. Pete was part of the syndicate and I had to stick with him no matter what he looked like.

I stood with my back to Pete for twenty seconds, maybe longer, then I turned back around.

"Forget about it," I said. "It's not important."

"You scared me there for a second," Pete said. "I really thought you were losing it. Come on, why don't you sit down? Take a load off."

I sat down on the bench next to Pete. I noticed that he was wearing cologne today, probably to cover up his B.O., but he'd put on so much of it he smelled as bad as he always did—maybe worse.

"I think I get what's going on," Pete said. "You think I was making fun of you. Well, I wasn't. I think you look great in that suit and with those sunglasses on— like a movie star. I also think it's good that you got dressed up today. It shows you're serious about this. That's what I wanted when I got into this thing—not just to be with guys who wanted to fuck around, for a tax write-off. I wanted to be with guys who wanted to get into the horse business to win. Come on, no hard feelings, right?"

I looked over. Pete was holding out his hand, waiting for me to shake it.

"No hard feelings," I said. I shook his sweaty hand, but I still hated him.

"I'll tell you what—when the horse is ours, when we come for the first time he races, I promise I'll wear a suit too. How's that?"

"Whatever," I said.

I was looking away again, hoping Pete would go back to reading his *Form* and forget about me.

"By the way, I wanted to ask you, where did you get those shoes?"

"Macy's," I said.

"Macy's?" He said. "You should've come by my store, I would've gotten you those shoes for a quarter of the price. Eh, it doesn't matter. Next time."

Pete was trying to make some more conversation. I stopped paying attention, but he didn't get the message. He kept talking to me, not caring if I was listening to him or not. I didn't know why Pete got to me so much. Yeah, he smelled and, yeah, he dressed like a slob, but there was more to it than that. Then it hit me—he was low class. I was sick of low-class people.

A few minutes passed, then Alan, Steve and Rob came up the escalator together. I guess I should've expected it, but I didn't. They were all wearing suits at the Chinese restaurant so I figured they'd look at least as good today. Steve and Rob looked about as slobby as Pete—in jeans, sneakers, and sweatshirts. The only one who looked halfway decent was Alan, but even he didn't look as good as he did the other day. He had a black shirt tucked into chinos and he was wearing shoes, but he wasn't wearing a tie or a jacket.

As soon as the horse started making money I was going to take my share of the profits and buy my own horses. Then it was going to be *sayonara* to these losers. We all shook hands. Then Alan said, "Let's all congratulate Pete for putting on some cologne today." Everybody laughed except me.

Steve said to me, "So what are you, getting married today?"

"No," I said.

"Then what's with the ice-cream man outfit?" he asked smiling.

Everybody laughed again.

"This isn't an ice-cream outfit," I said. "It's a five-hundred-fuckin'-dollar suit."

"I was just busting on you," Steve said. "You look great. I mean I'm going to my nephew's Bar Mitzvah later and look how I'm dressed?" He waited a second then said, "Nah, I was just kidding. I got a suit in the car. I just figured I'd put it on in the bathroom at the temple."

I couldn't believe it. He had a suit in his *car* and he wasn't wearing it now? Some kid's Bar Mitzvah was more important than his first day as a horse owner? Was the guy out of his mind?

I was so shocked I had nothing to say. I just stood there staring.

Everybody stood around for a while, bullshitting. I didn't say anything until Steve turned to me and said, "You're not Jewish, are you, Tommy?"

"No," I said.

"I didn't think so," he said, "I mean with a name like Tommy Russo. What are you, Catholic?"

I nodded.

"Me too," he said. "So you got any plans for Christmas?"

"Christmas? When's Christmas?"

"In two days," he said

"Oh yeah, I forgot," I said. "I'll probably just hang out in the city."

"That's cool. Yeah, my wife and me are gonna head up to Massachusetts, to her sister's house. Bores the hell out of me—not Christmas, just being up there in the sticks, you know? It's up near Amherst, not far from New Hampshire. They have a dog track up there so I figure the day after Christmas I'll—man, what the hell happened to you?"

I'd taken off my sunglasses to pick off the crust in the corners of my eyes. The other guys were looking over now too.

"I had to break up a fight at the bar last night," I said.

"That's a pretty nice shiner you got there," Pete said.

"You should see what the other guy looks like," I said.

I wasn't trying to be funny, but everybody laughed.

I put my sunglasses back on. Alan, Pete and Steve started talking, and Rob said to me, "I was meaning to ask you—what's the name of the bar you work at on the Upper East Side?"

"Blake's Tavern," I lied. Blake's Tavern was a bar on First Avenue in the East Eighties, about twenty blocks away from O'Reilley's.

"Oh," Rob said. "The only reason I asked is because I heard that story on the news—you know, how that guy's wife was killed. He owns some bar called O'Reilley's."

"I heard about that too," I said.

"It was pretty fucked up," Rob said. "They said the Super Bowl pool at the bar was robbed a few days before. Guy got away with fourteen grand."

"I guess it's a good thing I didn't buy one of those boxes."

"You can say that again."

I interrupted whatever Alan was saying to Pete and said, "Don't we gotta go up to the Steward's office and put the slip in the claiming box?"

"Bill Tucker's taking care of that," he said.

"But shouldn't we go up there anyway," I said. "I mean what if he forgets to put it in?"

"He won't," Alan said, and he started talking to the other guys again.

I went to the bathroom. When I came out I saw a tall thin guy with curly gray hair standing with the other guys. I figured this was Bill Tucker.

When I came over Alan said, "And this is the fifth member of our little syndicate—Tommy Russo."

"Pleasure to meet you," I said, shaking his hand.

"Same here," he said. He had a strong Southern accent and, I was happy to see, he was wearing a gray suit.

"I think you're one of the best trainers in the business," I said. "I know a lot of people probably tell you that, but I really mean it."

I realized I was still shaking his hand, maybe harder than I should have. I let go.

"It's great to meet you," Tucker said, flexing his fingers. "Nice to have some fresh blood injected into the racing industry."

It was five minutes to post time for the first race. Rob, Steve and Pete went to bet, so it was just me, Alan, and Bill Tucker. I didn't like the way Alan was trying to hog the conversation, talking to Tucker about shit I knew Tucker didn't care about. So I cut him off and said, "So tell me, Bill—you don't mind if I call you Bill, do you?"

"Bill's fine."

"So tell me, Bill. You ever had horses run at Hollywood Park?"

"Sure. Once in a while I ship to the California tracks."

"What's it like there? I mean behind the scenes. You go to parties a lot, I bet."

"Sometimes," Bill said. "But I spend most of my time up to my ankles in mud."

"Yeah, but I'm sure you go to a lot of Hollywood-type parties."

"Once in a while…I guess."

"Yeah? You think I can go with you sometime?" I said.

"I don't know," he said. "I don't see why not."

The other guys came back from the betting window and Bill started talking to them. I wished Bill and I were alone, so I could get to know the guy.

Then Bill said, "Come on, I'll take you folks out to my box to watch the race."

We went in past the same usher who'd given me a hard time before. I gave him a big smile as I walked by and I could tell he felt stupid.

It was a nice day—sunny and warmer than it had been lately, probably about forty degrees. I probably needed a coat, but I didn't wear one to the track. It didn't matter—I was so excited there could've been a blizzard and I wouldn't've noticed.

I sat in the seat next to Bill and the other guys sat on the other side of him.

"So you think your horse has a chance?" my actress-girlfriend asked me.

"As good as any of the other horses, sweetheart," I said, puffing on a hundred-dollar cigar.

"But do you think he'll win the race?"

"I don't know if he'll win, but he'll run good. I know that."

"What do you want to do after the races?"

"I don't know. I figured maybe we'd go to that big party at Clint's house."

"I don't want to go to Clint's party, I want to go to Jack's party."

"All right, we'll go to Jack's party then."

Pete was in the aisle, passing by.

"Not gonna bet on the race?" he said.

"Nope," I said.

"Why not? She's five to one—that's not too bad."

"I don't bet anymore," I said.

Pete looked at me like I'd suddenly turned Chinese.

"Yeah, right," he said. "That's a good one."

"I'm serious," I said. "I gave it up—went cold turkey."

"Smart man," Bill said. "Nobody makes a living betting on this game."

"Yeah, well I guess I'm not gonna make a living at it then," Pete said, "because I'm gonna take this horse down."

Steve and Rob stood up and followed Pete.

"I'm not gonna watch this horse win and not have any money on it," Steve said.

"I'm game," Rob said.

"I have to use the john," Alan said. "On my way back maybe I'll just make a small wager."

He winked at Bill as he passed by.

"So lemme ask you something," I said to Bill when we were alone. "When we get this horse, when are we gonna run her again? I mean you're gonna put her in a race by next week, right?"

"I don't know about *that*," Bill said.

"What do you mean?" I said.

"Well, next week might be a little too soon," he said. "We'll have to see how she comes out of this race, then we might want to get her on the track a few times, get some works into her—"

"So why can't you do that by next week? I mean I've seen trainers run horses back two days after the claim."

"Yeah, and then they have to lay the horse up for six months because they ran him into the ground. No, we're gonna take it a little easier than that with Sunshine Brandy—especially because she's a filly. With the girls you gotta be a little more gentle than with the boys. On the other hand, I like what I've seen of this horse so far—I really like it. She has a nice easy stride, a good pedigree, a good age too. Filly, lightly raced. She didn't run as a two-year-old and when she turns four next year I think she'll really have an edge. Yep, I think this horse has a chance to do something in state-bred allowance company."

"And then we're gonna enter her in some big stakes races, right?"

"Well, we don't want to get ahead of ourselves now, do we?" he said. "I think we'd be happy if we got into allowance company and ran a couple of good races."

"Why would we be happy then?"

"Because that would mean the horse was running good. That's the most we could hope for, right?"

"No. The most we could hope for is for her to win a Breeder's Cup race."

"Well, that sure is ambitious."

"Why?"

Bill looked at me funny, like he was confused about something.

"You're only paying thirty thousand-plus dollars for this horse," he said. "A champion race horse costs a lot more than that."

"John Henry only cost about twenty thousand dollars and how many millions of dollars did he win?"

"John Henry was a rare exception. For every John Henry there're a thousand horses who don't win anything."

"Maybe this horse will be another John Henry."

"Unfortunately," he said, "I don't think that's going to happen."

"It will," I said. "You'll see."

Pete came back from betting and started talking to Bill. Bill's negative attitude pissed me off. Now I realized why he was always at the bottom of the trainer standings.

The horses were coming onto the track for the second race. I stood up and stared at Sunshine Brandy, the number three horse. Bill was right about one thing— she was in great shape, all right. She had big muscular legs, a nice shiny coat, and she was walking on her toes and her ears were perked up. I wished I had binoculars with me so I could get a better look. Pete must've been reading my mind because he said, "Want a better look, Tommy?" and he was holding out his binoculars for me.

"That's all right," I said.

Pete was a loser and I was afraid if I touched anything he owned part of him might rub off on me.

Alan, Steve and Rob came back from betting and sat in their seats. I was still standing up, watching the horses pass the grandstand in a line, each one next to a pony. Sunshine Brandy looked so much classier than the other horses, like she didn't belong on the same racetrack. She had a good jockey on her too—John Velazquez.

I glanced at the tote board—there were only six minutes to post time.

I sat down, but I couldn't stop looking at Sunshine Brandy. The race was six furlongs so the starting gate was on the backstretch, on the other side of the track. Velazquez was jogging her toward the gate now, taking it nice and easy, airing her out. Even from far away she stood out from the field like a champion.

The horses were going into the starting gate. I looked at the tote board—there was less than a minute to post. I stood up on my seat to get a better view. Then the track announcer said "They're off!" and Sunshine Brandy, with the pink and red silks, shot out of the gate like a bullet. It was like she was pulling Velazquez along, doing all the work. She had a three-length lead, but it was an easy three-length lead. If Velazquez wanted to, it was obvious he could've opened up five or ten lengths on the field and the horse wouldn't've even broken a sweat.

Alan, Pete and the other guys were screaming their heads off, but I was just standing there, watching. Rounding the far turn, Velazquez let it out a notch and, suddenly, Sunshine Brandy opened up five lengths on the field. She looked like she was running even easier than before. It was like this was a workout for her while the jockeys on the other horses were whipping and driving, trying to keep up. In the stretch, Sunshine Brandy still had that big lead and Velazquez still hadn't used the whip. He was sitting straight up on her with a stranglehold. She still had about a five-length lead, but to me she looked like Secretariat in the '73 Belmont—all alone on the track, a champ. Then, about fifty yards from the wire, she went down. It happened in a split second. Maybe she took a bad step, or maybe one of her legs just snapped, because she stopped short and Velazquez went flying over her head, landing on his ass, and then the hind legs of the horse went off the ground and the horse tipped over, just missing Velazquez.

Suddenly, the whole crowd went quiet. The other horses ran by, but nobody was paying attention to the race anymore. Everybody was looking at Sunshine Brandy, trying to stand up on three legs. It was obvious she'd snapped one of her front legs now—the bone was sticking out through the skin, all covered with blood.

For the first time since before the race started I

looked at the other guys. They were staring down at the racetrack in shock.

"I'm really sorry, fellas," Bill Tucker said. "I don't know what else to say."

"Don't apologize," Alan said. "It's not your fault."

"I still *am* sorry," Bill said. "I really am."

"What the hell are *you* sorry for?" I said to Bill. "You didn't know the horse was gonna break her leg."

"I know, I know, but I still feel responsible."

I slapped Bill on the back.

"Forget about it," I said. "Let's just thank our lucky stars the horse didn't finish the race. At least now we can take our money and go claim another horse."

Bill looked at me and the other guys were staring at me too. I wondered what the hell was going on.

"I'm afraid that's not the way it works," Alan said.

"What do you mean?" I said. "It's our money. We can do whatever we want with it."

"It's not our money anymore," Pete said. "According to rules, once somebody puts a slip in the claiming box to claim a horse and the race goes off, the horse belongs to the new owner."

I stared at Pete for a few seconds, then I started to laugh.

"That's a good one," I said. "You guys almost had me going there a second."

"It's true," Pete said.

"Come on, you gotta be kidding me," I said. Nobody was laughing. "What about all the insurance we bought? The insurance must cover this."

"The policy kicks in *after* the race," Alan said. "Unfortunately, Sunshine Brandy is ours now."

I looked over at Bill Tucker and I could tell by his face that they weren't bullshitting. Then I looked back toward the track. An ambulance had pulled up next to the horse and the workers were setting up the screen so the fans didn't have to see them give the horse a lethal injection. In a couple of minutes we were going to own a thirty-thousand-dollar piece of horsemeat.

Suddenly, I lost it. I remember screaming and cursing like a wild man, running through the grandstand, pushing people out of my way. Somehow I made it back into my car. Next thing I knew, I was driving out of the racetrack, going as fast as my car would go, running red lights and swerving. I pulled over on a side street and took deep breaths, trying to get a hold of myself.

The horse was dead. It was still impossible to believe. One second she looked like the best horse in the world, the next she was on the ground and they were getting ready to give her the needle.

I needed to unwind. I spotted a bowling alley on Rockaway Boulevard and I pulled into the parking lot. I bowled for about an hour. I was just letting off steam, tossing the ball down the lane on two or three bounces to the pins. Afterwards, I felt better, more like my old self. Bowling had cost eleven dollars and now I had only three dollars and some change left to my name. I'd have to figure out a way to get some more money soon, that's all. I knew I could talk Frank into giving me another advance on my salary, and then I'd have to figure out a way to get twenty grand, or however much I would need to buy another race horse.

It was a little after four o'clock. Driving over the Queensboro Bridge, I was looking forward to going to work tonight, getting my life back on track.

I exited the bridge onto First Avenue and headed uptown. I found a good spot near East Sixty-second Street and walked uptown, toward my apartment. Turning the corner onto Sixty-fourth Street, I noticed two cop cars in front of my building. I turned around and walked back toward my car, as fast as I could.

I had no idea how the cops had caught on to me and I didn't have time to think about it. I had to get away, maybe leave the city, then I remembered I only had three dollars and some change.

Avoiding First Avenue, I walked up Sixty-second Street to Second Avenue and headed uptown. On Seventy-first, I cut over two long blocks to York. The sun had set and it was almost totally dark outside. I went into the vestibule of Janene's building and rang the buzzer. She didn't answer. Afraid she wasn't home, I rang again, pressing down hard with my finger. Then I heard Janene say, "Who is it?"

"Tommy," I said, relieved.

"Who?"

"Tommy. You remember me, don't you?"

She didn't answer for a few seconds. I was about to ring again when she said, "What do you want?"

"I have a surprise for you."

"What?" she said, like she didn't hear me.

"A surprise," I said.

"What's the surprise?"

"If I tell you, it won't be a surprise, will it?"

She didn't answer. I rang again.

"What is it?" she said.

"I have your jewelry," I said.

Again, she waited a few seconds before answering. "I thought you gave it to a pawn shop."

"I did, but the guy bought it back and now I just bought it back from him. Come on, just let me up so I can give it to you."

"I'll come to the bar tonight to get it."

"But I have it here—right now."

"Why can't you bring it to the bar?"

"I wanted to apologize to you too. I'm in Gamblers Anonymous now and in Step 6 you have to apologize to the people you've wronged. It would really help me if I had a chance to apologize to you, face to face. Come on, I'll just come up for a minute then leave."

The buzzer rang.

I took the elevator up to her apartment on the sixth floor. I rang once and she opened the door, wearing jeans and a white sweatshirt.

"Hey, how are you?" I said.

I tried to kiss her, but she backed away.

"I don't have cooties," I said smiling.

"Where's my jewelry?" she asked.

"Aren't you gonna invite me inside first?"

"Do you have my jewelry or not?"

"Yeah, I have it."

I went by her, into the apartment.

"I was hoping you could lend me some money," I said.

"*What?*"

"Just a few hundred bucks. I'll pay you back tomorrow or the next day. I promise."

"Do you have the jewelry or don't you?"

"First lend me some money."

"I'm *not* lending you money."

"Why not? I paid you back last time, didn't I?"

"Get out of here—right now."

I spotted her pocketbook on a chair in the corner.

"Sorry to have to do this."

"What are you doing? Give that back to me—"

I stiff-armed her, trying to keep her away, but she kept coming after me. Finally, I pushed her and she fell down onto the couch. I found about twenty dollars in bills in one of the pocketbook's compartments.

"Don't you have any more than this?" I asked.

Janene was crying. I thought about searching her apartment for more money when I had a better idea. I took her bank card out of her wallet and slipped it into my pocket. I put the pocketbook back onto the chair.

"If you just lent me the money this would have been a lot easier," I said, "but I *am* going to pay you back."

I left the apartment. On the landing of the stairwell I felt dizzy and I saw myself tumbling down the stairs. I took the elevator down instead. I walked around the corner to the Chase bank on First Avenue and Seventy-second. I still had Janene's pin number memorized. I put her card in the machine and typed in the code. A receipt came out with a printed message:

TRANSACTION DENIED

Damn it—she must've called the bank already and put a hold on the account.

On my way out, I spotted a police car speeding up First Avenue. I ducked back into the bank and stayed there until the coast was clear.

I needed money—fast—and there was only one place to get it.

I walked over to Second Avenue, down to Sixty-fifth Street, then back over to O'Reilley's on First. Luckily, there were no cops there. Frank was working the bar and a couple of old-timers were sitting on stools, watching TV.

Frank saw me come in and he screamed, "Get the hell out of here! Right now, you son of a bitch!"

"Why? What's going on?"

"You sick piece of shit! You fucking scumbag!"

"What?" I said.

"I don't wanna look at your face anymore. Just get the hell out of here!"

"Look, I don't know what's going on," I said, "but I'm sure—"

"How long were you fucking her?"

"Who?"

"You know who—Debbie. My fucking wife!"

"Jesus, I can't believe you just asked me that," I said.

"No more bullshit!" Frank's face was red and he looked crazy. The two guys in the bar got up and left.

"No," I said. "I wasn't fucking Debbie. Jesus, what kind of guy do you think I am?"

"Fucking liar! My doorman saw you there—last week."

"I *did* go there one day—looking for you."

"Look, you son of a bitch piece of shit, I know you were there, so stop lying to me! You killed her didn't you?"

"Take it easy," I said. "I know you're angry, grieving or whatever, but you don't have to take it out on me."

Frank came out from around the bar.

"A cab driver said he dropped her off by your apartment the day she disappeared. Then, that night, a cop pulled you over in Brooklyn."

"It's not what it looks like," I said.

Frank came after me, beating his fists against my chest.

"Come on, take it easy," I said. "Chill out."

Frank kept beating me until he got too exhausted, gasping for air.

"Look, you have to believe me," I said. "I know how bad things look right now, but I think you know I'm a good person. You know I wouldn't kill somebody. You'll see—they'll find the real killer and then you'll forgive me. But don't worry, I won't hold a grudge. I know what you're going through."

"What did you come here for anyway?" Frank said. "Money? If you can't steal it, you have to borrow it from your stupid boss, right?" Frank took his wallet out of his pocket and started throwing bills at me. "Here, you want my money? You want my fucking money? Take it! Take it all!"

I started to pick up the bills when I heard loud sirens. I looked behind me and saw two police cars pull up in front of the bar. I was about to make a run for it—

maybe try to get out through the window in the kitchen—when I looked back at Frank. He was still throwing money at me, but he was slumping back onto a bar stool.

"Come on, buddy," I said, trying to help him up. "Hang in there. Just hang in there!"

I looked behind me and three cops were standing by the door with their guns drawn.

"Hurry up," I said. "Do any of you guys know CPR?"

"Put your hands up where I can see them!" one of the cops shouted.

"The guy's dying here!"

"Put your hands up!"

"For Chrissake. Look at him!"

"Now, asshole!"

"You gotta help him!"

"Get your fucking hands in the air!"

I looked over at Frank, who was staring right at me. A cop came up behind me and pulled my arms behind my back and cuffed me. Frank was slumped over on the stool, leaning against the bar.

"Will somebody help him, damn it? Forget about me. Help him!"

One cop went over to Frank.

"Hang in there, buddy," I said. "You just hang in there."

Frank was looking at me, his eyes half shut.

"Let's go," one of the cops behind me said.

"Don't die," I said to Frank. "Whatever you do— don't die. You have to make it out to Arizona, buddy. You're gonna love it out there."

"Come on," one cop said to me, and the other one said, "Move it."

I tried to turn around, to look at Frank again, but I couldn't.

"See you tomorrow!" I yelled as the cops pushed me out the door.

Get Hard Case Crime by Mail...
And Save 50%!

☐ **YES! Sign me up for the Hard Case Crime Book Club!**

As long as I choose to stay in the club, I will receive every Hard Case Crime book as it is published (generally one each month). I'll get to preview each title for 10 days. If I decide to keep it, I will pay only $3.99* — a savings of 50% off the standard cover price! There is no minimum number of books I must buy and I may cancel my membership at any time.

Name: _____

Address: _____

City / State / ZIP: _____

Telephone: _____

E-Mail: _____

☐ **I want to pay by credit card:** ☐ VISA ☐ MasterCard ☐ Discover

Card #: _____ Exp. date: _____

Signature: _____

Mail this page to:

HARD CASE CRIME BOOK CLUB
20 Academy Street, Norwalk, CT 06850-4032

Or fax it to 610-995-9274.
You can also sign up online at www.dorchesterpub.com.

* Plus $2.00 for shipping. Offer open to residents of the U.S. and Canada only. Canadian residents please call 1-800-481-9191 for pricing information.

If you are under 18, a parent or guardian must sign. Terms, prices, and conditions subject to change. Subscription subject to acceptance. Dorchester Publishing reserves the right to reject any order or cancel any subscription.